TWO
STREET

TOM LARSEN

MONTAG

First Montag Press E-Book and Paperback Original Edition September 2024

Montag Press ISBN: 978-1-957010-47-2
Design © 2024 Amit Dey

Montag Press Team:

Cover: Rick Febre
Cover photo: "Rooftops of Little Italy, South Philadelphia" by Trish Hamilton.
Author photo: selfie by Tom Larsen.
Editor: Lindsay Krumbein
Managing Director: Charlie Franco

A Montag Press Book
www.montagpress.com
Montag Press
777 Morton Street, Unit B
San Francisco CA 94129 USA

Montag Press, the burning book with the hatchet cover, the skewed word mark and the portrayal of the long-suffering fireman mascot are trademarks of Montag Press.

Printed & Digitally Originated in the United States of America
10 9 8 7 6 5 4 3 2 1

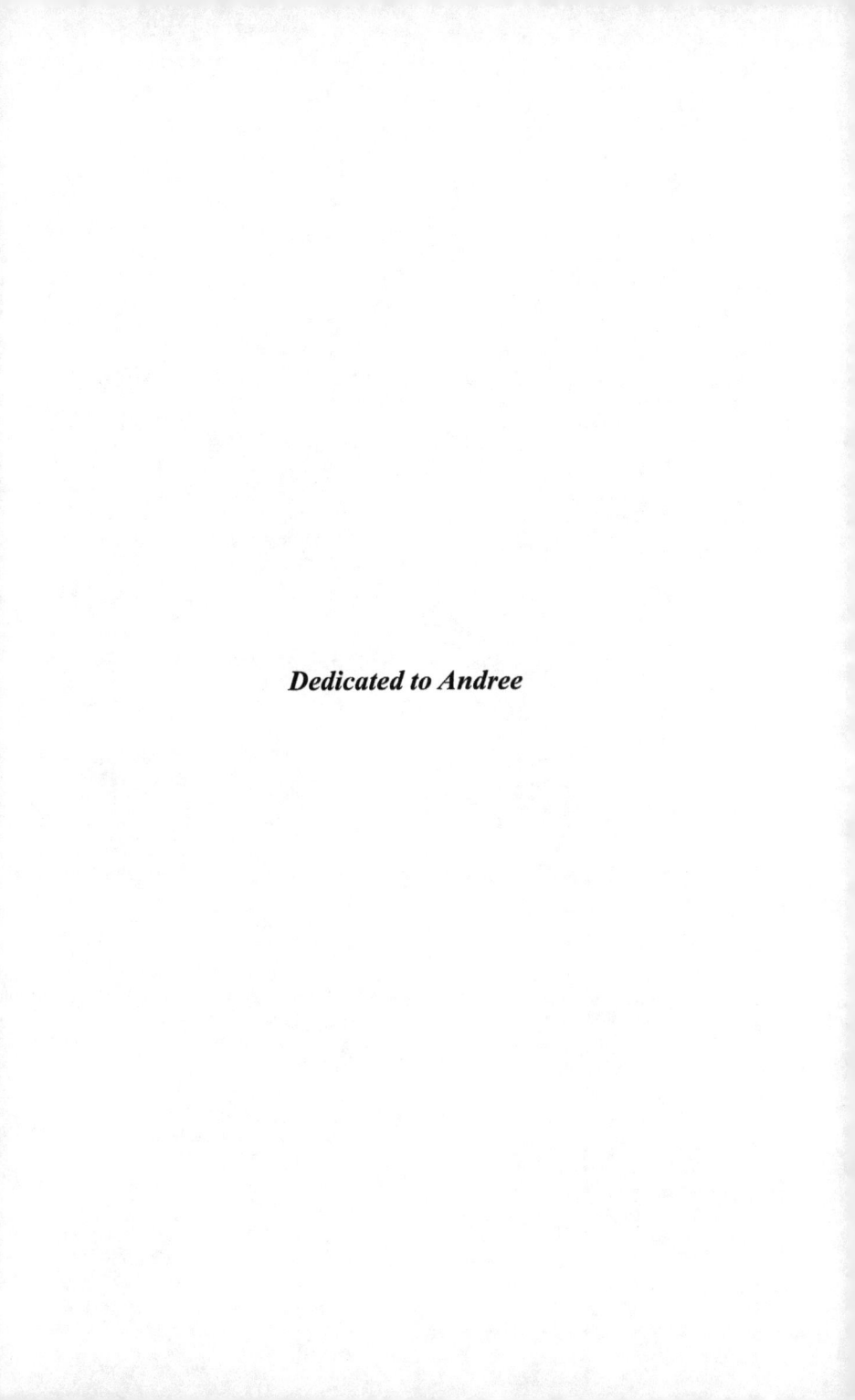

Dedicated to Andree

TABLE OF CONTENTS
AND PUBLISHING DETAILS:

All the rights to my stories have reverted back to me.

TRACER

It was cold the first time I saw him. The temperature had dropped steadily through the day and by the time I walked over to pick up Gina at the hospital the sidewalks were slick with ice. The dog stood in front of Silvio's like he expected someone to come out. He was big and dopey and when he looked my way the word "hangdog" came to mind. He was still there when we came back and at Gina's insistence, we crossed the street to avoid him.

That night it snowed half a foot. I woke to the unmistakable scrape of Donnegan's snow shovel under my window. Donnegan's an early riser and has been known to clear half the block before anybody's up. He's convinced this vigilance enhances his standing in the neighborhood, but mostly we feel guilty about it. Apparently, I feel the guiltiest, since I'm the only one who lends a hand.

We were just finishing up when I saw the dog turn the corner. He moved down the odd side of the street sniffing the stoops, sometimes circling back to double check. His fur was matted and he walked with a limp. Before I could say anything

Donnegan gave a loud shout and the dog slinked off with a whimper.

I told Gina but she shrugged it off. Lost mutts don't make her priority list. For the rest of the morning I pictured him roaming the streets, searching for one familiar thing. I've heard stories about pets that overcome insurmountable odds to find their way home, but this one didn't look the type. When I lived in Berkeley the dogs seemed as independent as the people and it wasn't unusual to see a Lab or a Golden Retriever poised on the corner, waiting for the walking light. Around here dogs that run loose end up on a reward poster.

I didn't see him again for two days. By then the outside spigot had burst and you could ice skate on the puddle in my yard. I was lugging frozen trash to the car when I spotted him outside the rectory pawing through a plastic garbage bag. I watched him burrow in until his nose poked a hole in the bottom. A minute later the housekeeper came out with a broom and gave him a whack. His hind legs spun over the ice like in a cartoon.

I knew I should say something. But what?

That night I lay in bed listening to the wind rattle the storm windows. I couldn't stop thinking about the dog. I see the bums on the subway grates downtown, but I don't lose sleep over them. I give my share to the deadbeats and free-loaders, but I don't worry about them when it gets cold. Gina says the dog is probably sick or the owner kicked him out, but I don't think so. The thing about a lost dog is he has this look, part fear but mostly confusion. He just can't figure it out. All he can do is keep moving and hope for the best. I know what this must feel like.

I've owned one dog in my life – an Irish setter named Katie. She was what you call excitable. The guy who sold her to me claimed she was housebroken and at times she was. Katie's devotion to me was slavish to the point of embarrassment. Even after she was grown she would insist on jumping in my lap when I got home. At night she slept under the covers and her galloping dreams and sighs of contentment kept me up half the night. Katie was crazy but everyone loved her. Once, she disappeared for a week and I fell apart worrying. When the SPCA called to tell me they'd found her, I was on the third day of a binge. The guy at the desk had his reservations, but the way she slobbered over me convinced him to let her go.

She was one of those dogs who loves to ride in the car with her head out the window. I can still see her grinning into the wind like some great auburn hood ornament. The wind made her sneeze, which made riding in the back inadvisable. One summer I drove her all the way to California, effectively curing her of cars forever. I left her for an hour in a motel room in Cheyenne, Wyoming, and when I got back, she was sitting in a glass strewn parking lot howling at the moon.

My last year in California I gave Katie away to a hippie with a ranch in Sonoma. To this day I can't believe I did that to her. I often wonder if she's still out there, and if she'd remember me after all these years. As long as she could still be alive, I guess I'll wonder. Some dogs live to be twenty, which gives me four more years to torture myself.

I decided to call the animal shelter first thing in the morning, but by the time the guy showed up to jump-start the car, I'd forgotten all about it. I've a lot on my mind these days. In three weeks my unemployment claim runs out and I don't think the car will make it through the winter. To top things off the credit card bill came yesterday. The clank of the mail slot is starting to get to me.

I never should have gone to Brennan's in the evening. Here I am out of work and I'm buying rounds like some high fucking roller. Then Pete Myers told me the Allen kid was bitten by a dog over on Mifflin Street. He said folks were up in arms and the dogcatchers had been called in. I know that Allen kid. Whatever he was doing, he got what he deserved. Pete said he'd blow the dog's head off if he caught him in his trash again. They're not big on strays around here.

I knew I'd be up all night worrying. I was the dog's only hope and that made me responsible. Every way I looked at it came out the same. Either I'd do nothing or go find him. Take him out to the country, or worse, bring him home. Do nothing and he'd freeze to death or the dogcatchers would put him down. Hell, they'd be doing him a favor. Poor mutt had probably never even been to the country.

I should have gone straight home, but instead I walked around in the cold thinking I might see him somewhere. I ended up on Federal Street where the crazy lady feeds the cats. Must have been a dozen of them hanging around waiting. Someone always takes care of the cats. After a few minutes she showed up with a ten-pound bag of cat food in a shopping cart. I asked if she'd seen the dog, but she pretended not to hear me. We watched the cats jockey for position. Their breath came in little steam clouds, but they didn't look cold. Most of them lived in the abandoned buildings along Second Street, something a dog could never get away with.

More snow. This time I let Donnegan knock himself out. I'd been taking the battery out of the car at night, which meant I got to dabble with tools twice a day in the freezing cold. I wasn't cut out for winter. Sometimes I spend the whole day watching television, and when I look out the window I can see Wilson across the street watching his and old Mrs. Mokowski watching hers. Even with the thermostat cranked up it's always cold in the house. Gina walks around with a half dozen sweaters on and at night she wraps herself in blankets.

After supper I went down to Ernie's to play my number. The wind hit me head-on at the corner, and by the time I got there my face was on fire. I had a shot of brandy and listened to Ernie rag on the Republicans. He's had the place for as long as I can remember. Last summer he put a For Sale sign above the awning, come spring he'll be retiring to Florida. Sold enough rotgut to kill us all and bows out to a life of leisure. It won't be the same around here without old Ernie.

The wind was still howling when I started for home and I pulled the drawstring on my hood as tight as it would go. Past the pizza place I saw something moving on the sidewalk and as I drew near, I could hear the scrape of claws on the pavement. The dog was in bad shape. When I knelt to brush the snow from his face, he didn't even turn his head. I looked for a tag, but there was only a broken hook hanging from his collar.

Down the street I heard Donnegan and Pete Myers yowling at each other, and behind me the 5 bus rolled by without stopping. I picked up the dog, wrapped him in my coat, and started walking.

He sleeps next to the heater in the basement. The deal I made with Gina is this: we will not take the dog to the vet. We will give him a warm place to sleep and a chance to recover. The rest is up to him. I am solely responsible for feeding and changing. He'll have to be in diapers until he can walk. Gina didn't enter into the agreement willingly. I had to beg and plead and in the end, simply refuse to carry him back upstairs. She threatened to have her brother do it, but Ricky would never tangle with me.

The dog sleeps on an old carpet remnant left over from the bedroom. He's too weak to stand, but when I put food near his mouth he eats, and when I give him water, he drinks. I haven't given him a name yet. Naming him will only diminish his chances. If he remains anonymous he will survive.

I spend most of my time in the basement these days. Sometimes I read to him from the paper. I know he's listening by the way his ears swivel. When Gina comes home I try to talk to her, but she answers in a way that only leads to silence. I know this isn't what she had in mind when she married me. Throw in the dog and it's a wonder she speaks to me at all.

Wednesday I go to Jersey to see about a job. I know it's Wednesday because Ernie's is closed and I have to walk three blocks for cigarettes. The guy in Jersey takes an instant dislike to me. I'm a journeyman machinist, but my age and the gaps in my resume are starting to work against me. Some of my references have been out of business for years. Work in a few places that go belly up and employers get gun shy. He especially doesn't like the money I want and tells me so, which pretty much kills my enthusiasm. With twenty years in the trade why should I work for nothing?

On the way home I buy thirty bucks worth of lottery tickets. I must be losing my mind.

The dog managed to turn over while I was gone. I take this as a positive sign. Except for an occasional groan, he still hasn't made a sound.

At night I think about him safe and warm. Helps me sleep. Gina wants to know what I'll do if he recovers, but I can't think that far ahead. She complains the house smells like dog, but it doesn't really. The house smells of cigarettes, fried onions, and thirty years of Mrs. Sullivan's boiled cabbage. The old girl passed away shortly after she sold us the place, but the smell lives on. Donnegan claims his mother raised seven kids on boiled cabbage and potatoes. They leveled the old neighborhood years ago but he swears he can still smell cabbage in the empty lot.

Some things I've noticed about my basement. The way the clothesline is strung through holes in the beams, the elaborate network of plumbing. When Gina flushes the toilet, I can follow the water all the way to the street. A date stamped on the side of my furnace tells me it's older than I am. Except for not heating the house, it's never given me a problem. Every July

I fire it up and let it run for a while. I heard somewhere that this is good for your furnace. In winter the basement is the warmest room in the house, and in summer, it's the coolest. When we moved in I threw out most of Mrs. Sullivan's stuff, but over the years we've managed to fill it with our own. Crap we'll never use. Boxes unopened for ten years.

"They dug this basement in 1917," I tell the dog. "Mick Irish. Working stiffs. Dry as a bone down here. Not like the basement where I grew up. You wouldn't like it there, kiddo."

The fuse box and meters are in the far corner. Every month a skinny black girl takes the readings, slips in and out without a word. What does she see in all these basements?

Donnegan has identified the green stuff on my pipes as asbestos. He says Mrs. Sullivan's son-in-law tried to take it off, but botched the job. Donnegan is adept at spotting shoddy workmanship. He urged me to have the asbestos removed as soon as possible. Last summer when he asked about it, I told him I had the pipes replaced. Now I can never let him back in my basement.

There's a light switch between the ceiling beams, but when I flick it nothing happens. The basement has a single window set at street level. When the neighbors are outside I can see their legs and shoes. The kids scurry by on Big Wheels, never thinking to look over. For the past month the window's been covered with snow. When I open it the square of white is as smooth as glass, so I draw a happy face with my finger.

"1917! The year the Bolsheviks killed the czar. Woodrow Wilson was president, and Bullet Joe Bush was pitching for the A's."

The dog considers this.

"There were men around who fought in the Civil War. Wyatt Earp and Sitting Bull were still alive. Lindbergh hadn't crossed the Atlantic."

I've been spiking his water with vodka. It's an extravagance, sure, but something like that can keep you going. He seems to like it. He's able to prop himself on his elbows now, so I slide the bowl under his chin. I clean up his messes right away so Gina can't complain. She makes a big deal out of doing the laundry, muttering curses as she clomps down the stairs. I don't think this is good for the dog, but I keep my mouth shut. It's another argument I'd never win.

The furnace kicks on with a low whoosh. There's a chrome handle on top with an arrow pointing down. When I turn it, the front opens. Inside the door is a list of maintenance tips demonstrated by a generic white man with thinning hair. Here he is kneeling with an old-fashioned oil can. Here he is removing some sort of filter. The tips mention nothing about running the furnace in the summer.

I can hear Gina moving around in the kitchen. We spend her days off ignoring each other. When we first met, I was working in the Navy yard. I had a motorcycle and a goatee. Gina was recently divorced and just entering nursing school. From the beginning, we were determined to do it right, to learn from past mistakes. We didn't count on different mistakes.

I should never have shaved the goatee. It gave me the sort of menacing look that can anchor a personality. Without it I'm just another guy turning into his father. The goatee might have gotten me hired the other day. Who knows how the goateed guy will handle rejection.

Gina leaves without saying goodbye. I sit in the basement doing crossword puzzles. Last night the dog took a turn for the worst. His breathing is shallow and there's yellow scum in the corners of his eyes. It looks bad, but what do I know? A shot of antibiotics and he might be as good as new.

In the afternoon, I bring the TV down and turn the dog so he can see. We watch old movies until Oprah comes on. It occurs to me that if the dog dies I'll have no excuse to come down here.

"Here's one. Dr. Adams – trauma – emergency care."

The dog whistles his indifference. I fold the Yellow Pages in my lap and punch in the number. The receptionist answers with a mouthful of food.

"Yeah, hi. Listen, my dog is breathing funny."

"Mmmmph, - sounds serious. Better bring him in right away."

"He's got yellow gunk in his eyes."

"Not good."

"Are these symptoms of anything in particular?"

"You'd have to ask the doctor. Shall I schedule an appointment?"

"But you said it's not good. So you've seen this before?"

"I have an opening for tomorrow morning."

"Let me get back to you."

The receptionists at Doctors Burger and Cappelini shed no further light, so I pick the closest. Capellini can see us today.

A pair of dachshunds charge when I open the waiting room door. Forty little claws skitter over faded linoleum. The dogs huff and growl, then beat a hasty retreat when I step inside. Their owner, a beefy blonde, doesn't even look up from her magazine. As I cross the room, the dachshunds scatter in opposite directions, then converge in a teeth-rattling collision. Stupid animals, dachshunds.

I sit in a corner with the dog draped over my knees.

Cappelini must be in his seventies. As he lowers an ear to the dog's chest, I can hear them wheezing in tandem. He tells me it's an upper respiratory infection, then staggers off in a coughing jag.

"What are his chances, doc?"

"You should have brought him in sooner," Cappellini growls. "I'm a doctor, not a magician."

"Yeah, but what do you think?"

"Let me examine him. You wait outside."

The beefy blonde and I sit smoking in the waiting room. No one enters, and no one leaves. The dachshunds never take their eyes off me. I flip through a magazine, registering nothing.

"Sir?" the receptionist calls from the sliding glass window. "Can we have your dog's name for our records?"

"He hasn't got a name. I just found him in the street. I figure I'll wait to see if he makes it."

She gives me a sympathetic smile.

"You know what's a good name? Tracer. You know, like those bullets that glow in the dark? I don't know why, but I always liked that name." She taps a nail against her tooth to encourage me.

"I don't know. It sounds like a young dog's name."

"He was young once, you know. I got an Uncle Skip who's almost eighty."

"OK then, Tracer it is."

She types in the name, then leans back to have a look.

It snowed again last night. When I got up, Tracer was spread eagle on the couch, snoring like an old man. He's had the run of the place since Gina moved back to her mother's. For the past two weeks I've been driving a cab for some outfit out by the airport. It's not so bad. When the weather breaks I'll probably take the dog along, but for now, I leave him at home with the TV on. The thing about dogs is they don't expect much and they don't hold things against you. They're just glad to see you is all.

LIDS

Timothy "Lids" Picone has always been partial to the smell, but this guy is too much. Eight, ten times a day he hears him hacking his lungs out. Minutes later he can smell it right through the fucking wall. Stanley calls him the pothead, or sometimes just "the pot." Picone doesn't see how the guy can function. But he does function.

The walls are so thin he can pick up everything with his stethoscope. He's heard some things he'd like to forget. The pothead really plays the roll, flashy clothes, flashy car. His sound system could do serious structural damage. Sometimes Picone has to plug his ears to sleep at night.

It's been three weeks since he moved in. Stanley put up the deposit, but the rent came out of Picone's pocket. It should be well worth it. Every Friday night, the pothead checks out with an empty duffel bag, and when he comes home, the bag is full. The rest of the week is traffic, all hours of the day and night, mostly yuppies and college kids. Funny how dopers look like everyone else these days. Except for Maurice. The dreadlocks and gangster shades are a dead giveaway. Droopy eyelids just like Picone's. The droopy lids make Maurice look dangerous.

Picone's just make him look sleepy. All things considered, it's better that way.

Maurice usually arrives with an entourage and a lizard skin attaché case. Might as well have "Drug Dealer" stenciled on the side. Picone can hear the snap of latches through the wall. The pothead's door and windows are wired, and he has a wall safe in his bedroom. Picone's heard the tumblers clicking.

According to Stanley, the pothead and Maurice are planning a major transaction. Cocaine by the kilo. Picone wishes they'd get on with it.

He eats the rest of the tuna salad while working on the Matterhorn. Seven completed puzzles are spaced over the living room floor, separated by pathways. As he works Picone listens to classical music on the radio. His attention is perfectly divided.

He got into the puzzles while he was at Rahway. For a time he had them all over his cell, but the guards broke them up in a roust, and then the cons started stealing pieces just to aggravate him. Funny that he had to wait until he got out of the joint to do his puzzles in peace. He knows them by heart and each one triggers a different response. Childhood memories that refuse to focus. Love affairs that never happened. He studies the pattern of bark on a pine tree in the foreground. The mountain and the lilting strains of a violin combine to bring tears to his eyes. He can cry at the drop of a hat.

Sometimes he dreams about taking a trip around the world to visit the actual sites of his puzzles. The farthest Picone's ever been from New Jersey is Las Vegas, two years ago on a job. He saw a Vegas puzzle in a casino gift shop – an aerial view of the Strip at night. But it was an old one. Sammy Davis was still at the Sands.

His favorite is the one of the Golden Gate Bridge towers poking up through the fog. He can stare at it for hours. Fog so thick you could scoop out a hunk and stick it in your pocket. He used to wonder how the photographer knew it would be that way, but then Stanley told him the fog rolls in like that all the time in Frisco. Stanley's been around. In fact, Stanley was one of the cons who would steal his puzzle pieces. He claimed the puzzles were making Picone crazy. Stanley ought to see this.

The pothead turns his television on. The tinkly piano of "The Young and the Restless" comes through the wall and in less than a minute Picone smells the reefer. Like clockwork, this one. An hour later the fat girl with the jangly bracelets shows up, and then three yuppies in business suits. The doorman must be on the payroll.

In the afternoon, Picone walks down to play his number. On his way back, he runs into the pothead coming out of the building. They smile and exchange nods.

"You're the new guy in 312," the pothead says.

"That's right."

"Jack Mercer," he reaches for Picone's hand. "I'm your next-door neighbor."

"Lou … Lou Dorsey."

"Listen Lou, I've been meaning to tell you. If it gets too loud in my place, just give a thump on the wall. I know how thin those walls are. The guy before you had parrots. It was like living in the goddamn Amazon."

"No problem. I don't hear so good."

"Great! I mean for me. Hey, why don't you stop over some time? Have a beer."

"Thanks. Maybe I'll take you up on that."

"OK. Look Lou, I gotta run. If you need anything, just let me know." He reaches again for Picone's hand.

"Will do."

Mozart and the Matterhorn. Picone imagines himself living in a cabin with a view of the mountain. Not that he's much of an outdoorsman. The one time he camped out he slipped a disc and ended up in traction. He drops a section of the tree in place and takes a deep drag on his cigarette. The box advertises other mountain puzzles, including Mt. Rushmore in South Dakota. Picone tries to place South Dakota on his mental map, but the middle states just run together. When he was a kid, his family moved to Ohio for a few months after his old man jumped bail. He can never remember the name of the town, but it always seemed to be raining there.

He turns off the radio during the daily Sousa program. Minutes later he hears the elevator door open and the jangle of keys next door. It takes a while for the pothead to unlock all the locks. When he's inside, Picone hears him latching latches and turning dead bolts. What a joke! You could put your fist right through the door.

This morning he took the old name off his mailbox and replaced it with Lou Dorsey. No sense giving the guy a reason to be suspicious.

The moaner drops by and for the rest of the afternoon he is forced to listen to the pothead hammer her into the headboards. He likes to think she's faking it. During a break in the action he makes a pot of tea and slips a pizza into the microwave. Hanging around an empty apartment would drive most people crazy, but Picone doesn't mind. He admires the sociability of others, the pothead for instance, but he doesn't envy them. Stanley's the closest friend he's got and Picone can't stand the sight of him.

He eats the pizza standing at the kitchen window. The shadows of the buildings stretch across the street and he can hear the traffic light switch above the intersection. He watches the Asian woman from the grocery store arrange bulbs of garlic in the window. This part of town used to be Italian, but the Koreans and Vietnamese have taken over. The old pisanos piss and moan, but Picone figures if they wanted it, they never should have sold it.

Up the hill, he hears the bells from St. Anthony's chime four o'clock. Further up he can see the old bleachery water tower. When they were kids, Petey Falcone dared him to climb the tower. He can remember Petey sprawled in the grass below, growing smaller as he pulled himself up the ladder. From the top, Picone could see the whole city, and he was startled by how shabby it looked. A place where nothing good ever happened. Even the trees looked dirty. He circled the narrow catwalk for nearly an hour. When he finally climbed down Petey was gone. Picone never went back there, and in thirty years nothing good ever happened.

A sudden knock on the door scatters his thoughts. It's the pothead, looking casual in linen pants and a silk shirt.

"Howdy neighbor. Mind if I come in?"

"I'm uh, kind of busy right now. Can we make it another time?"

"Hey, no problem. Listen Lou, I'm having some friends over later. Maybe you'd like to stop by?"

"Tell you the truth I haven't been feeling well lately. The doctor says I need some rest."

"Gee, I'm sorry to hear that." The pothead tries to see inside but Picone blocks his view. "Tell you what, I'll see if I can switch this thing to another location. Give you some peace and quiet for a change."

"Ah hey, you don't have to do that. I'm one of those guys who can sleep through anything."

"I insist. Really, it's no problem. It's about time somebody else cleaned up the mess."

"I appreciate the offer, but don't bother. It won't make any difference to me."

The pothead heaves a sigh. "To tell you the truth Lou, I'd give anything just to sack out in front of the tube for an evening. Sometimes I get sick of the whole business."

For a moment he really does look sick of the whole business, but then something shakes him out of it. He tells Picone a Polish joke and a story about someone named Bernie on the seventh floor. Picone feels foolish standing in the hallway. The pothead is making an overture of some kind, but Picone can't figure it out. Is he queer? Does he suspect something?

"Lou Dorsey ... that's a great name. A movie star name. My real name is, get this, Angus. Can you believe it? Parents are cruel, man. I mean life is hard enough, right?"

"You don't look like an Angus," Picone assures him. The guy must suspect something, but what? Picone hasn't left the apartment for days, except to lay in supplies. Maybe that's it. A world beater like the pothead would find that strange. It is strange.

"You know, you do look a little under the weather, Lou. Ever try vitamins? I've been taking them all winter and haven't had a sniffle."

"I guess I've been a little shaky since the operation."

"Jesus Lou! You should have said something. Now I'm definitely moving the party to Greta's place."

"Seriously, you don't have to bother."

"It's no problem. She lives three blocks away. Believe me, I know what it's like to be laid up. I broke my leg skiing last year. Nearly went crazy stumbling around my apartment for three months."

Picone steps back inside hoping to cut him off, but the pothead just keeps rambling. He pushes the door halfway but the pothead moves in closer.

"Give this a try, Lou." He hands Picone a thin joint. "Might not cure what ails you, but you'll be too blitzed to care."

Picone waves him off but the pothead reaches over and drops it in his shirt pocket.

"Maybe you'll change your mind later. If nothing else, it will help you sleep. Plus, you can watch almost anything on TV," he gives a wink. "Just don't try to program your VCR."

Picone stands with his hand on the doorknob, looking down at the twisted end of the joint in his pocket.

"Thanks. Listen, I'll talk to you later, OK?" He steps inside, and quickly shuts the door.

Stanley calls.

"We're on for Friday evening, Lids. The Kelleher's will be at their daughter's for the weekend, so you won't have to worry about them. After the deal, Mercer and the nigger should be celebrating at the Club Cabana until the wee hours."

"How do you know they'll leave the money here?"

"We're talking fifty grand, at least! What, do you think they'll have it on them?"

"What if they take it to Maurice's?"

"The nigger lives in the badlands. Besides, Mercer went to the trouble of having a safe installed. He'll want to use it."

"He wants me to come over and have a beer."

"You talked to him?"

"He stopped me in the parking lot and introduced himself. What could I do?"

"That's terrific. Did you tell him you were gonna rob him?"

"I told him I was Lou Dorsey and I just had an operation."

"Jesus. I don't believe this! Look, I don't wanna know, OK? Just remember, Friday night. The Kellehers will be away. You should have most of the night."

"Tell me Stan, where do you get your information? All of a sudden you're like the fucking CIA."

"I know somebody. You gotta know people, Lids."

Martha Kelleher is carrying groceries in from a waiting cab when Picone returns from the diner. He tries to slip past, but the old girl stumbles into him at the door.

"Need a hand with those, ma'am?" he offers.

"Why thank you, young man. I declare, that doorman hides when he sees me coming." Her voice is warm and grandmotherly. Picone balances a bag in each arm and follows her into the elevator.

"I live on the third floor," she tells him.

"I know. I'm your new neighbor, Lou Dorsey."

"So, YOU"RE the Wagner aficionado." She taps his wrist. "I can't tell you what a relief it is to be rid of the last one. Tell me Mr. Dorsey, you're not a bird lover, are you?"

"Not me." He struggles to push the button. "I don't think my Dobermans would go for it."

Mrs. Kelleher stiffens.

"Just kidding," he grins.

What's with the charming routine? For weeks he didn't speak to anyone but the waitress at the diner, and now he's hobnobbing with the neighbors. Stanley would frown on this.

"My husband loathes Wagner. I must admit I find him a bit bombastic myself." Mrs. Kelleher's smile gives a hint of former beauty.

"It's just the radio," he confesses. "I'm afraid I'm not much of a music buff."

They step off the elevator into a cloud of marijuana smoke.

"This is an outrage!" Mrs. Kelleher waves a hand in front of her face. "My husband says to ignore it, but the man has no shame!"

"Aw, it's not so bad. Reminds me of my youth."

"Oh, you're just teasing." Another tap to the wrist. "Anyone can see you're not involved in such things. You must come in and meet my husband. You can tell him about the Dobermans."

"No really, I'm expecting a phone call."

"Nonsense, we're right next door." She leans over the doorknob, patiently fitting key to lock. When the door swings open, a slight, white haired man is crouched in the doorway clutching a cast iron skillet.

"Gracious Walter, you were right there! Why didn't you open the door?"

"I thought you were being robbed," he says sheepishly. The skillet slips from his hand and crashes to the floor between his feet.

"And what were you going to do dear?" Mrs. Kelleher brushes past him. "Console me with an omelet?"

"Why no. I was going to leap to your defense."

"Oh Walter, you're just like that old man in the hijack movie. The heroic one, remember? Those terrorists swatted him like a fly."

Picone's not so sure. He has, in fact, been cold cocked by just such a skillet during an ill-advised burglary some years earlier. His attacker was in his eighties. He sets the groceries on the counter and steps away.

"I really should be going."

"You must stay for tea," Martha waves him away from the door. "Walter, this is the young man who was playing the Valkyries the other night. Our new neighbor, Lou Dorsey. Mr. Dorsey? Walter."

"Mr. Kelleher," Picone offers his hand. The old man steps over the skillet to take it.

"My boy, it's a pleasure to meet you. I hope you'll excuse the paranoia, but it's not like Martha to bring a handsome young stranger home," Walter chuckles. "I don't know what I intended to do with that frying pan, but I'm sure it would have been a humiliation for all of us."

"Walter is a physical wreck," Martha explains, herding them along. "I'm surprised he made it all the way to the kitchen without his walker."

"She's making that up. The walker part anyway." Walter gives him a pat on the back. "Although I must admit I've seen better days."

"Oh, he could go any time." Martha takes Picone by the arm.

In contrast to his place, the Kellehers' apartment is crammed with furniture. Bookcases and curio cabinets line the walls. They make their way around coffee tables and davenports to a set of facing sofas. Walter and Picone each take a sofa. Martha hesitates for a second, then settles next to her husband.

"Any pets, Mr. Dorsey?" Walter asks.

"No birds. I already checked," Martha answers. "Tell him what you said, Mr. Dorsey."

"Aw, I was just being a wise guy." Picone blushes.

"He said a bird would disturb his Dobermans.'

Walter stifles a groan.

"He was only teasing." Martha slaps his thigh.

"Walter and I are from Holland originally. We eloped to America when I was eighteen. You know something, Lou? We never looked back." Martha nods emphatically. They are into their second round of brandies and Haydn is playing ever so softly above their conversation. Picone wonders what happened to the tea.

"You didn't like Holland?" he asks.

"It's a lovely country, but we were young and ambitious. Walter saw himself as a New York gadabout, jumping in and out of taxis. I planned to spend my life shopping."

"You did, dear," Walter reminds her. "You see Lou, when people come here for the first time, they generally assume we moved here from a large house. That would explain the abundance of furniture. This, however, is not the case. Our Manhattan apartment was smaller still. Martha sees a room as something to be filled."

"I was preparing for a real home someday, but alas ..."

"I've never met a Hollander before," Picone tells them.

"The Dutch have a way of blending in," the old man gently corrects him. "You probably know dozens without realizing it."

"Did you live near the windmills?" Leo conjures his puzzle.

"As a matter of fact, we did." Martha scoots to the edge of the sofa. "Walter and I lived near the sea. His town was twelve miles from mine, and every evening, he would ride over on his bicycle, right past the windmills."

They replay the scene in their heads, smiling serenely. These two are a riot.

"What do you do, Lou?" Walter arches an eyebrow.

"I'm in restaurant supplies." Picone gives his standard response. It's a line of work he could see himself in if he wasn't boosting apartments or doing time. It's also something he can bullshit his way through in a pinch. His cousin Dom is in restaurant supply, and all he does is bitch.

"That sounds dangerous." Martha tugs at the hem of her dress.

"Dangerous?"

"Well, the papers say the restaurant business is run by the mafia. Those gangsters from Philadelphia."

"The papers say everything is run by the mafia. It saves a lot of leg work." Picone quotes his cousin directly.

There's a painting lit by a brass lamp above Walter's head. A night scene – the shadow of an old barn set against a moonlit sky. From where Picone is sitting, the moon appears luminescent. He gets up to take a closer look, but the effect is the same from any distance.

"Cadmium," Walter pulls a pipe from a rack built into the sofa.

Picone leans in closer. "In the paint?"

"A popular, but imprudent artistic experiment. The man who painted that picture is said to have died from toxic poisoning."

Picone backs away. Through a gap in the drapes, he can see a slice of the city in the fading light, a skewed version of his own view. Behind the washstands, cabinets, and common wall lies another world. Picone's world, empty and wasted. An enormous craving for furniture rises within him. Forty-eight years old and nary a couch. What does this say about him? Loser. Convict. Not a single lamp or painting. He lived in a flophouse for two years before moving here, but when he tries to envision his furnishings, he gets only vague shapes and general locations.

"My grandparents came over from Palermo in 1924," he hears himself say.

"Well then, they must have come through Ellis Island, as we did sixteen years later." Walter scrapes at the bowl of his pipe with some sort of instrument.

"My grandfather was a mortician. He worked on Dutch Schultz and Fiorella La Guardia."

Is he crazy? Why is he telling them the truth? His mother grew up in a house filled with stiffs. His grandfather worked into his nineties, and toward the end, his own deterioration did little to comfort the bereaved. Rather than follow in his in-law's footsteps, his own father turned to crime. In the end, the old man sold the business and gave his money to the church. The new owners kept the name. Venuto's. Picone feels a chill every time he passes the place.

"Walter and I have decided to be cremated when the time comes," Martha says. "Our daughter has agreed to keep our ashes on a particular shelf above the radiator in her den. Frankly, the idea of moldering away is very distasteful." She wrinkles her nose. "This old body has been good to me, and to throw it in a hole when I'm done seems downright disrespectful, if not barbaric."

"The older you get, the more funerals you're obliged to attend," Walter adds. "We've been to a dozen in the past two years, and I must tell you, I always shudder when they lower that box into the ground."

"Yes. How can we do that to them?" Martha wonders.

"And I, for one, get no consolation from the fact that my flesh will provide nourishment to the lower life forms," Walter grumbles. "It may be natural, but it lacks dignity."

"Twin Cloisenait urns for us, right Walter?"

"Dignified."

Martha opens a tin of shortbread cookies and offers them to Picone. As darkness falls, she traverses the room, angling gracefully around secretary desks and uncornered corner cabinets to light assorted stained glass lamps. The soft glow makes Picone want to kick off his shoes.

"My grandfather talked to the dead," he blurts out. "He would address them by name as he worked, and if he asked them a question, he would pause long enough for them to answer." All true. "The living didn't really interest him. My grandmother actually ran the business."

"Ridding the world of its dead." Walter sighs. "A lucrative profession."

"But your poor mother, growing up in a mortuary. I don't see how that could be healthy." Martha clutches at her collar. Picone thinks back to periods of refuge in his grandfather's house. He never once saw a body, but he knew they were there, draped in shrouds in the basement. When Petey Falcone died of leukemia, Picone's grandfather handled the embalming personally. In deference to the family, he made Petey look better in death than he ever looked alive.

"The way I figure it, when you're dead, it really doesn't matter what they do with the body." Picone shrugs. "It isn't you anymore, it's just meat. The thing you gotta remember about cremation is it takes a while. It's not like they just pop you in the oven. They gotta cook it for a while."

Martha winces. "Is that true Walter?"

"I suppose so, dear. It is rather a large … er, piece of meat."

"Well, I never imagined the exact procedure." Her face clouds for a moment. "Oh, I don't care. It's not like you can feel it."

"Who's to say?"

"Stop that Walter. You know how anxious I am about this. Besides, I already bought the urns."

"Why doesn't that surprise me?"

"I'd take this a little more seriously if I were you, Walter. After all, you're the one who's hanging by a thread. Perhaps I'll just have YOU cremated and see how it goes."

"That would be the wise thing."

"You could always freeze him," Picone suggests.

"Heavens no!" Martha shudders at the thought. "The idea is to avoid the cold. We want to be comfortable, you see."

Walter fires up the pipe, and for a moment his head disappears in a cloud of smoke.

"Spending eternity in an urn might prove tiresome," he points out.

"They're lined in satin. I used the lining from one of your old violin cases."

It turns out that Walter Kelleher was a violinist in the Philharmonic orchestra before arthritis forced him into a well-furnished retirement. For the next hour, he reflects upon a life of travel and culture unknown to the likes of Picone. He tells colorful anecdotes about symphony screwballs and society geezers, and describes the world's great concert halls in vivid detail.

"You don't strike me as the Wagner type," he jabs his pipe in Picone's direction.

"It was just the radio."

"The man was a fascist. The most insufferable egomaniac ever to draw breath,"

"It was just the radio."

They have progressed to the scotch and Martha's cheeks have taken on a distinct glow. The old timers can really put it away. Picone knows he should leave, but is unsure if he can even stand. Walter steps effortlessly over to a framed photograph and hands it to him. The picture shows a stately brick building with a young Martha poised on the top step.

"The Academy of Music in Philadelphia," he says. "On the evening this picture was taken, Pincus Zuckerman nearly lost an eye to a broken violin string. Martha and I had just moved here. And this," he points to a slash of white tail fin at the pictures edge, "is my Caddy. For a time, I was the automotive trendsetter in residence."

"How long ago was that?"

Walter lights a match and holds it to his pipe.

"Well, let's see. We moved here in 1968, so that would make it twenty-eight years. Of course, the neighborhood has changed considerably. First the Asians, and now the movers and shakers. They're thinking of turning the building into condos, you know."

"No, I didn't."

"Can you imagine taking out a mortgage at our age?" Martha rolls her eyes. "We've decided to move if they force us to buy. Of course, moving will probably kill Walter."

"I think we should just sell everything and sponge off the children for a few years." Walter replaces the photograph.

"Listen to him, a few years. And then what Walter?"

"Oh, I don't know. Retire to Alaska?"

"Alaska? The idea is to get away from the cold."

"That's when we're dead, dear. While I still live and breathe, I intend to distance myself from my fellow geriatrics."

Picone marvels at their patter. Most of the old people he knows have outlived their sense of humor. He wants to hear more about Holland and the symphony, and possibly a bit more about their daughter, who is, judging from various photographs, a younger version of her mother. But just as he's slipping off his shoes, he hears a telephone ring in his apartment.

"I'd better be going," he struggles to rise. Before he can straighten up the ringing stops. He smiles and settles back into the sofa. Walter chuckles and fusses with his pipe.

"You know, Lou, Walter still has that Cadillac." Martha breaks the silence. "It's been sitting in a garage for almost fifteen years."

"A classic overindulgence. I'm afraid we became very attached, the caddy and I." Walter shakes his head. "I intended to have it completely restored, but the automatic transmission self-destructed and then, before I knew it, a decade had passed. Even now, I envision Martha and I rolling across the desert to parts unknown."

"That's my husband for you," Martha sighs. "I don't drive and he's one scotch away from cerebral hemorrhage. Did you have a particular desert in mind, dear?"

"As a matter of fact, I was thinking of Death Valley, the wildflowers in springtime. It's the kind of place old men dream about when they realize their limitations."

"Take a pill, Walter. It'll make you feel better."

It's nearly eleven when Picone drags himself away. Martha sees him to the door, and rises on her toes to peck his cheek.

"Thank you so much, Lou," she whispers. "We get so little company these days. I haven't seen Walter this animated in years."

"I think I might know somebody who might want to buy that Cadillac, Mrs. Kelleher."

"Oh goodness, I don't think Walter would ever sell."

"This guy is crazy for Cadillacs. He'd pay top dollar, depending on the condition. Tell you what, why don't you give me the address where it's stored, and I'll take a look at it."

Martha glances over her shoulder, and steps into the hallway.

"It's at 227 Walker Street," she tells him. "I'm afraid it wouldn't be worth much after all these years."

"You never know. This guy's loaded."

The moaner arrives at the pothead's an hour later. Through the peephole, Picone sees her pacing and hears the impatient snap of chewing gum. The pothead answers the door in a burgundy kimono. A real piece of work, this guy. Picone returns to the Matterhorn, listening as they gush over each other. Their enthusiasm undermines his solitude and he finds himself losing interest, even as he fits the jagged peak in place. For lack of anything better to do, he goes to the kitchen to fix a sandwich. As he bends to search for the mayo, the tiny joint falls from his pocket and rolls beneath the refrigerator. He hesitates for a moment, then kneels to retrieve it.

From the window he can see the old marquee of the Strand Theater. He remembers riding in the car, listening to his father describe the old landmarks – the dancehall turned into a tire outlet, the dry cleaners where the cigar shop used to be. Old places gave way to new places in those days. Now there is nothing to replace the past. It stays to haunt you, crumbling in front of your eyes. The Strand has been boarded up for more years than it was open. The dry cleaners and tire outlet are long abandoned. Anchored to empty neighborhoods, they fade, but refuse to fall. Picone has walked these streets at night, moving through the shadows like a ghost. When he was a kid he was always afraid, but now he just feels sorry for himself.

One time they broke into a building over on Fourth Street that turned out to be a lodge meeting hall. They found uniforms and funny hats, and in a back room, wonder of wonders, a steamer trunk filled with gleaming sabers. For weeks they played pirates under the Baker Street bridge until Danny Burns' mother called the cops. The papers dubbed them the Baker Street Buccaneers, and even ran a picture of Danny with the sword jutting from his belt. The old lodge burned down while he was in prison. Danny Burns retired from the police department ten years ago.

He watches a show about hydrocephalus. The narrator explains that the brain continues to function even when compressed against the rim of the skull. He has the computer graphics to prove it. Picone hangs on his every word. He switches to a program about alternative energy sources, and marvels at the logic. The CNN business report makes perfect sense.

Stan drops by in the morning to check on him. He sees the puzzles through the doorway, pushes past Picone and walks the narrow path to the center of the room.

"Un-fucking-believable! If I didn't see it with my own eyes, I wouldn't think it was possible."

"Yeah well, I'm trying to get it out of my system." Picone scratches his head. "There isn't a hell of a lot to do here, Stan."

"What's this?" Stan points to a puzzle with his shoe. "I think I've seen this one before."

"That's Pompidou Center. It's like an art museum."

"Looks like somebody turned it inside out."

"It's in France."

"The thing is, this makes me very nervous, Lids. Here you're schmoozing with Dopey next door, and now you're doing the place in wall-to-wall puzzles. Think you got enough fingerprints here?"

"What do you think, I'm gonna leave them behind?"

"I don't know what to think. Why not just spray paint your name and address on the wall?"

"Hey Stan, don't get your bowels in an uproar. Just worry about your end, OK? I open an empty safe and you owe me big time."

Stanley moves over to the window, straddling the Roman Coliseum to look outside.

"This is like one of those stories you hear on the corner, Lids. You know, local bungler takes a fall. Don't forget I have my reputation to consider."

"So give me a grand, and we forget the whole thing. It's all the same to me."

Stanley steps away from the window, edges his foot beneath the Coliseum's upper rim, and sends the pieces flying.

"It's a matter of professionalism. Understand what I'm saying?" He sidesteps over to the Grand Canyon. "Fraternizing with a mark is unprofessional. This …" he kicks the Canyon halfway to the ceiling. "… is not professional."

Picone doesn't flinch. Stanley's capacity for violence is a matter of record. As the beefy ex-con begins demolition on the Acropolis, Picone settles in the corner to watch.

"As for forgetting about it, forget about it." Stanley flings whole sections of the temple his way. "Friday night you go to work. When you're finished, you check into the airport Holiday Inn. I'll meet you there Saturday morning. It's a cakewalk, Lids, in and out. You do this right, and we move on to bigger things."

"Anything else, boss?"

"Yeah. Scrub the place down. Every handle, every door, every fucking thing. They lift a print outa, here and I promise you'll never make it back to Rahway."

"What's that supposed to mean?"

"Hey, it ain't just me homeboy. I got partners. The only thing these guys like more than money is whacking guys like you."

"Partners? What do you think I'm going to find in there, Stan?"

"Whatever you find, you grab it all." Stanley crouches next to Picone, balancing on the balls of his feet. "Listen Lids, we go back a long way. I know you're a stand-up guy, but you're a little flakey sometimes, know what I'm saying? I worry."

Picone rolls his head into the corner.

"If you got partners, how come I gotta lay out eight bills?"

Stanley rises and tends to the crease in his pants.

"Think of it as an investment, Lids. Come Saturday, you'll have more money than you can count."

227 Walker Street is a walled-in cinderblock building rimmed in razor wire. Inside, a half dozen uniformed mechanics

huddle over assorted dismantled vehicles. Picone approaches a wiry Asian with a cigarette dangling from his lower lip. The Asian directs him to a fat man with mutton chop sideburns.

"Kelleher?" the fat man looks him over. "You mean that piece of shit Caddy? You want it? I'll give it to you."

"I want to know how much it would cost to restore it."

"Kelleher. Jesus, he must be in his eighties by now. What's this, a second childhood thing?"

"He doesn't know about it. I want it to be a surprise."

"It's a surprise alright. I woulda junked that boat years ago, but the old guy sends a check every month for storage."

"How much?"

"Sixty bucks. OK, it's a little steep, but it ain't like I hold a gun to his head."

"To fix it. How much?"

"Jesus, I'd have to check it out."

"Would ten grand do it?"

"Oh yeah, we could do a nice job for ten grand. Not mint, of course, but very nice. Say, who are you, his kid? Kid Kelleher? Hey Lee …" he calls to the Asian. "You ever hear of Kid Kelleher?"

Lee mutters an obscenity without losing the ash on his cigarette.

"I'm just a friend," Picone says. "Is the Caddy here?"

"Yeah sure, it's in the back."

Picone follows the fat man to a back room – "the morgue," as he calls it. A handful of vintage gas guzzlers sit shrouded in dust, at the far end, the Caddy. No serious body damage, no rust.

"Say, uh …" Picone glances at the name above the fat man's pocket. "Vince. Let me ask you something. For fifteen grand can we roll this off the assembly line, or what?"

"Fifteen grand and you got yourself a cherry Cadillac, Mr …?"

"Dorsey. Lou Dorsey. So, Vince, when do you think we could get started on this?"

The fat man shakes his head.

"Well, I'll be honest with you. We're booked for a good two months. With all the hotshots moving in I got my hands full."

Picone paces the length of the room marking the silence with each step. He pauses at a gutted '57 Chevy, shoves his hands in his pockets and heaves a dramatic sigh. When the tension has reached the proper level, he turns to the fat man and cups his hands to his chest, a la Corleone.

"Like you say, Vince, the problem here is Mr. Kelleher is getting on in years. Did I mention that I'll be paying cash?" He repockets his hands, and retraces his steps until he is standing in front of the sweating fat man.

"What would another grand get me, Vince?"

"Another grand would put you at the top of the list, Mr. Dorsey."

"I won't forget it," he takes the fat man's hand, squeezing just hard enough. "I'll be around Saturday morning. What time you open here, Vince?"

"Usually 8:30, quarter to nine."

"Nine it is, Vince. Ciao."

Friday night Maurice arrives carrying a suitcase in lieu of the attaché. Nostrils flaring with greed, he nods to the pothead and leads him through the handshakes before stepping inside. Picone can barely hear them at first. Moving along the wall with the stethoscope, he tracks them through the living room to the bedroom. More locks, a dropped key, mumbled curses, and then they're inside.

"Come on, let me look at it," the pothead sputters.

The snap of suitcase latches is followed by a muffled scream, then two muffled screams. Stanley has stepped in it this time.

"Put it away, put it away," Maurice squeals. "No, don't touch it, don't touch it." His unseen histrionics send the pothead into belly laughs.

"We're rich. We're freaking rich," they shriek in whispers.

Picone makes himself a sandwich while they blow off steam.

Midnight comes and goes. Sprawled on the carpet, smoking one cigarette after another, Picone endures a litany of delusions and pipe dreams culminating in a Maurice island fiefdom crawling with nasty bitches. His prurient interests revived, the pothead calls a cab to take them to the Cabana Club. The whine of tumblers sets off a medley of keys, locks, and shrill giggles fading down the hallway and into the night. Picone waits for fifteen minutes then heads to the closet for his tools.

On his knees, he runs the box cutter blade over the wallboard in a low arch, deep, but not deep enough to be heard. He retraces the cut line again and again, moving left to right. After twenty passes he changes the blade and reverses direction, slowly, methodically. A thin layer of dust covers the carpet, the scattered puzzle pieces, and the tops of his shoes. By the second pack of blades, the carved out section begins to work lose. A dozen more strokes, and the blade pierces the wall at the top. Straining to be quiet, he pulls out the hump of sheetrock in one piece. The inside studs are placed a foot apart. Plenty of room. Stuffing a blanket in the gap between the walls, he uses the cross beam as a straight edge, cutting parallel lines in the inside wall, connecting the lines with a cut along the cross beam. He works in a catcher's crouch, bracing himself with his free hand. He's done this sort of thing before. Patience is the key.

When the cut line is paper thin, Picone rocks on his backside and kicks out a perfect triangle. It lands on the pothead's bedroom carpet with a soft thud. The safe is centered on the far wall in a square patch where a picture should be, a toy with ten digit tumbler. He wedges a crowbar in the seam, and pops it open.

Stanley calls at 2 am. Picone can hear the screech of brakes on a passing bus.

"What's going on, Lids? I'm going nuts here."

"I'm just getting started. Our boys left about an hour ago."

"It's a cakewalk, Lids," Stanley insists. Picone fingers a wad of bills, picturing a frosted cake with Betty Boop legs.

"Go to bed, Stan."

"By this time tomorrow we'll be Atlantic City. I can see us, Lids. I can see us so clearly it scares me. I don't know what it is man, but whenever I get this close something always screws up. Tell me nothing is gonna screw up, Lids. I need you to tell me."

"It's a cakewalk, Stan. Just like you said."

"Jesus, I got heartburn like you wouldn't believe. I can't get comfortable, you know? It's like I wanna crawl out of my skin. Sometimes I think it was better inside, Lids. No pressure, you know?"

"You need to relax, Stan. Take a bath. Fix yourself a stiff drink and soak awhile. It works for me."

"Yeah right. If I try to do anything, I'll forget to worry, and then we're in trouble. I swear to God this stuff makes me nutso."

"You could always come over and help."

"I can't let anyone see me there. I shouldn't even be calling. You know how far I had to walk to find a phone booth that works?"

"Let me go to work, Stan."

Picone runs his finger along the map from the expressway to the Turnpike, then west to the interstate. The names of the towns run together like a morning traffic report. He remembers a class trip to Valley Forge when he was a kid, and the time his parents stopped at Hershey Park on their way to Ohio. Dayton. That was the name of the town. His single Dayton memory is of his father sideswiping a station wagon, then berating the driver as his mother pleaded. From Pittsburgh he can catch a flight to Frisco. Find a nice place with a view of the Golden Gate Bridge. Picone closes his eyes and pictures the furniture in his future – a roll top desk with secret compartments and tiny keys, a solid mahogany chest of drawers.

On the way out he tapes a note to the pothead's door.

See Stanley. Black Lexus. Airport Holiday Inn. 8 am. Love, Lou

"How do I look dear?"

"Positively rakish!" Martha reaches over to smooth a silver sideburn. Rakish indeed. In his tweed cap and Ray Bans, Walter is the picture of senior chic. He conceded the white ascot and cigarette holder at Martha's insistence, but then Walter has long deferred to Martha's sense of style.

"You look like an older FDR," she tells him.

"I feel like a new man, by God. A rambling rogue full of spit and vinegar." He takes her hand, and brings it to his lips. "I can only think it's a miracle. The angel Lou Dorsey sent to us in the eleventh hour."

"A bolt out of the blue."

"And the timing, Martha! The exquisite confluence of fate. I must confess, at first my euphoria was tempered with regret for the lost years."

"You sure had me fooled, leaping around like an old baboon."

"Now I see it as a fitting conclusion to lives well lived. A finale of the grandest sort."

"I just pray he's not in some sort of trouble."

"The boy's a pistol, Martha," Walter pounds the steering wheel for emphasis. "I didn't think they made them like that anymore."

They lose themselves in silence as the miles slip by. At the freeway interchange Walter bears left and heads the old Caddy into the sunset.

PSYCHED

Wipers hammer the hood, but Lena can barely see. Just blurred taillights through sheets of rain. The car ahead tails the car ahead all the way up the line. If the lead guy drives off a cliff, they'll all be along directly. Jaws of life, she can't stop thinking. Jaws of life doing what they do, ripping and prying open. Oh, sweet Jesus, spare me the jaws.

"So, those bozooms ..." shock jock pauses for effect. "They are real, no?"

"That's right. What you see is all me."

"Oh my."

"Do you like them?"

"I am madly een love with them. Especially thees ... nono, thees one."

Lena turns it up a tad. She's been listening for over a year, casually at first, but now she hates to miss him. It's not something she's proud of, but a little titillation seems to suit her in the morning. That there are women who will do that sort of thing on the radio. Somehow the radio makes it steamy.

"And your husband, he does not mind that you bare your breasts for lecherous strangers?"

"On the contrary. It really turns him on."

A trucker blows past in a rolling fantail, and Lena bids him a fiery death. Another mile, and she exits at the hospital. The old trees cut the rain to a trickle.

"And when I get home? You know what the first thing he'll want to do?"

"Tell us, my leetle cupcake."

Lena parks and listens until the commercials. Turning it off is like breaking a spell. As she stares out at the puddled grounds, a wave of weariness washes over her. Six years Lena's been at the nuthouse, and nothing she'd walk into would really surprise her. Then it's out the door, heels crunching across the lot. She tries to conjure a tranquil scene, but she's tried that before and it never works. Up the front steps at a perky trot, through the doors, and into the bedlam.

"... so you can march his black ass right back out of here." Alice goes hands on hips at a cop who looks fresh out of junior high. Behind them, two more cops wrestle with a huge, frothing guy. To their right, Big Dot yells into the phone, face knotted in fury. Patients mill around in varying degrees of agitation, and behind them, a maintenance crew gathers outside, looking in.

"Lutheran says they're full up," the young cop sputters. "What am I supposed to do? Chauffeur him around all night?"

"What's the problem?" Lena steps up to the plate.

"This one wants to kill his brother." Alice rolls her head at frothing guy. "Some hanky panky goin' on, but I can't make sense of it."

"Get a hold of Doctor Herbert," Lena pushes through. "Tell him it's an emergency. Does he have a medical card?"

"Um-hmmm." Alice breezes past with a snicker. "Piece of the Crock. With the, uh, Fool coverage."

"Sentinel? I thought they went under. … OK, call to clear admission and have his records sent over. Anyone know what he's on?"

"Had a pocketful of these." Dot holds out a half dozen crack vials.

Lena takes kiddie cop aside. "Tell me officer, what exactly did Lutheran say when you brought him in?"

"The usual, short-staffed, no beds. Nobody wants the bruisers."

"And they told you to bring him here?"

"They suggested it. You're on the list."

"I wonder if you could do me a favor in your travels today. If you should run into any more loonies," Lena touches a finger to his wrist, "just look the other way. Could you do that for me?"

The kid swallows a grin. "Be a pleasure, ma'am."

Lena takes a clipboard from the desk and hands it to Dot. "Have them take big guy to the green room and stay with them until the doctor arrives. Alice? Get me Lutheran on the phone."

Lena drops her umbrella in the bin and checks the discharge board. A nervous little man comes up beside her.

"Nurse Watts? I hate to bother you … I know you're very busy."

"How are you, Mr. Robbins." Lena forces a smile.

"I'm OK, I guess. It's about the lizards in my room?"

"Lizards? Are you sure they're not cockroaches?"

"Oh, they're lizards all right." Mr. Robbins wrings his hands. "Blue ones, about three inches long. At night I can hear their tails scraping the floor."

"Do you suggest we kill them?"

"They keep me awake."

Lena hooks his arm and walks him toward the common room. "But they ARE lizards, Mr. Robbins, and quite rare in Philadelphia. Personally? If a family of rare lizards chose to live in my room above all others, I'd feel a little bit special."

"But their tails … scrape, scrape, scrape."

"Tell you what. The exterminator will be coming to check on the elves in Mrs. Tully's air conditioner. I'll send him over."

The little man heaves a sigh. "Oh, thank you Nurse Watts."

"No problem, Mr. Robbins." Lena hands him off into psycho orbit.

"I have Lutheran on the phone!" Dot hollers over. Lena grabs the nearest phone, and drops into the nearest chair.

"Admissions? Yes … Freddie hi, I'm fine and you? … Well, actually I'm calling about the ball buster you dumped on me this morning … right … Save it Freddie, you're out of your league … How about one fire alarm away from a wacko invasion … Oh yeah? Try me. I got a guy who will chew your nose off. I got stalkers with no one to stalk. I got blowtorch killers, acid throwers. I got a freaking cannibal. Do yourself a favor Freddie, next time make a few calls."

"Line two. Sentinel Insurance Group." Alice punches the speaker button. "Girl, you are gonna love this."

"Nurse Watts speaking."

"Um, hello?" a small voice, clueless. "Can I speak to Mr. Thaddeus Johnson, please?"

"Mr. Johnson is tied up at the moment. Is there something I can help you with?"

"Is Mr. Johnson exhibiting suicidal tendencies?"

"Mr. Johnson wants to kill his brother."

"Um, what would you call that?"

"We call it homicidal?"

"… I'm sorry, homicidal is not on my list."

"Your list?"

"I have hallucination and hypertension, but no homicidal."

"Try under "N" for nuts."

"… … No, nothing. And it's a really long list."

"Oh, dear what shall we do?"

"I'm only authorized to approve things that are on my list."

"Tell you what. I'll just send Mr. Johnson over. See what you can make of him."

"… Me?"

"Would you mind?"

"But we're in Atlanta."

"That way we can get him out of our hair and you can make your own diagnosis."

"… In Georgia?"

"Let's pretend you agree to take him."

"Maybe you should speak to my supervisor."

"That would make YOU suicidal. Now look at your list there under 's'. See it?"

"… uh-huh."

"OK then I'll need an admission form, and Mr. Johnson's medical history, including allergies. Think you can do that for me?"

"My boss is gonna kill me."

"That would make HIM homicidal. You might want to add that sucker to the list." Lena hears something crash in another room, then it's Big Dot bellowing from the hallway.

"YO LENA, THAT CREEP SANDERS JUST SHIT IN THE TRASH CAN AGAIN!"

Six years, in June. It didn't start with psych. Juvee drug disorders had been Lena's first choice. At the time, it seemed to make perfect sense. She'd been a juvenile for years, and between school friends and her sister's crowd they had the drugs covered. It would be just like high school, only she'd get paid for it.

But these weren't like kids she knew. They came from crummy homes with crazy parents, and it took all the drugs they could take to get through it. Not so much recreational, as occupational. After that, she worked detox, another logical progression. Lena's first husband was a junkie, so she knew those ropes from bottom to top. But the crackheads were so needy and obnoxious she wanted to take a hammer to them.

Six years on a psych unit. She likes to think she's seen it all.

The elevator opens on an obese patient with a goofy smile and a massive erection. Alice locks on Lena's arm.

"Mercy!"

Lena reaches to hold the door open.

"That's very good, Dennis. Go show Dot."

"Be still my heart!" Alice fans her face with a clipboard.

"Charlie!" Lena calls over her shoulder. "Get Dennis his Hustler before he locks himself in the mop closet."

Down the hall, Eddie sticks his head out. "Yo Lena, Henry Walters wants to see you as soon as you get a chance."

"Who the hell is Henry Walters?"

"New CEO. Third floor, west, you can't miss it." He gives a wink. "Big dollar sign on the door."

Samuel L. passes by on a white man rant. Doughboy sputters curses into an invisible cell phone. Loopy Lu lip synchs Streisand since the others complained. Tish the Tramp shuffles past, clucking like a chicken. Lena looks to Alice.

"You heard. When I get a chance."

"I'm thinking, September."

"2050."

The morning passes in a noisy blur. Maintenance men shatter a fluorescent light, setting off a spastic stampede. NASCAR roars all afternoon, and Larry the Lip stabs the Shadow with a ball point. Standard stuff, run of the mill.

"Anybody seen Dennis Carney?" Eddie pages the lunchroom. "Lena?"

"He was in the lobby this morning, waving it around,"

"And forget what they say about white boys, honey." Alice waves a hand. "That one has the apparatus."

"Why Alice Long, I do believe you're smitten," Eddie cackles.

"Well, how crazy can he be? Maybe you could learn to live with it."

Dot squeezes past them rolling her eyes. "They want you upstairs right away, Lena. Mr. Powers That Be?"

Lena looks to Dot. "How about this guy? What, he's got an early tee-off?"

"Be nice," Big Dot warns her. "Heads are rolling."

Henry Walters studies the Titleist logo, picking away at the lint from his pocket. He is tall and tweedy, richly tan, and silver at the temples. He palms the golf ball as Lena enters, and gestures to the chair facing him.

"Ah, Mrs. Watts."

"Mr. Walters."

"Have a seat, please."

"That's OK, I can't stay."

Walters slips the Titleist in his pocket. "Mrs. Watts, it's a real pleasure to meet you at last. Tell me, how long have you been here at General?"

"Six years in February … and you?"

Walters smiles weakly. "You are aware that the hospital has undergone a change in management."

"Oh, I'm aware all right."

"Miss Watts, it has been brought to my attention that certain staff members disapprove of these changes."

"That's Mrs. Watts, and I can't say I'm surprised."

"I'll come right to the point. There have been an inordinate number of complaints regarding, shall we say, the abrasive attitude of the nurses on the detox unit. Yourself, in particular."

"I wouldn't take them too seriously."

"I DO take them seriously. In fact, I have no reason to doubt the veracity of these complaints. I might add that your confrontational reputation precedes you."

"Think of it as a low tolerance for stupidity."

"Yes, well, as head of personnel I've decided to assign John Strickland to oversee detox operations. Mr. Strickland and I feel that an alignment is necessary to ease budgetary constraints. This assignment will go into effect immediately, and continue until such time as a determination can be made about the program's viability."

"Strickland?"

"That's right."

"With the pocket pal?"

Walters squirms slightly. "Mr. Strickland is the Efficiency Coordinator and Operational Liaison for the Metro Medical Group."

"Do tell."

"I sense a note of hostility, Mrs. Watts."

"Let me get this straight. Metro thinks that detox is a money hole. As an 'efficiency' measure, management will appoint a six-figure bean counter to deal with malcontents. What else? … Oh yeah, any confrontational or abrasive behavior will be dealt with severely. How am I doing?"

Walters taps his fingertips together. "I'm curious, Mrs. Watts. Do you like working here?"

"Is that a requirement?"

"According to your evaluation, your former superiors thought quite highly of you."

"My former superiors were in the medical profession."

"Meaning?"

Lena shrugs. "Their primary concern wasn't turning a profit."

"Can I tell you a story, Mrs. Watts?" Walters drums his hands on the armrests. "Several years ago, a promising young surgeon applied for a position over at Mount Sinai. The hospital courted this particular doctor with the aim of setting up a first-rate cardiac program. It was a controversial courtship, in that many on the staff believed the money could be put to better use. The hospital persisted, despite a number of significant resignations."

Lena stares holes in his skull.

"But this doctor was a thorough young man. He looked into fiscal projections, and concluded that, given labor unrest, the hospital couldn't afford him. In the end, Mount Sinai lost their doctor and at last report, is now poised on the verge of bankruptcy."

Full bore lasers right between the eyes.

"You see, Mrs. Watts, as distasteful as it may seem, profit margins fuel the medical industry. This is a fact of life. Metro didn't invent the system, but we fully intend to prosper in it."

Lena holds a few beats.

"That's a terrific story. Now I've got one for you. There's a kid downstairs, Randy Hewitt? I don't expect you know him, but he's a good kid. A little paranoid sometimes, but he knows the program and he's making progress. In fact, he's doing so well, his insurance company is switching him to out-patient."

Walters sneaks a peek at his watch.

"Now anyone familiar with his situation can tell you that Randy isn't ready, but tomorrow, we have to discharge him, another fact of life, but one that won't show up on your pie charts and bar graphs. This morning I found a note in my mailbox. Randy wishing ME good luck. Can you beat that?"

Traffic going home is even worse. Road turned to river, cars flying off like it's paved with banana peels. By the Acme she sees a girl that looks like Marilyn off the shoulder by a car with a crumpled hood, Marilyn at twenty-one, a thousand years ago. Ten, at least, since they found her frozen in the woods, so it couldn't be Marilyn, but Lena checks the rear view anyway.

She watches TV, a cop show, something about identity theft she can't follow. Her regular programs have been pre-empted by March Madness. Lena so loathes March Madness.

She listens to her husband snoring softly. Would he mind if another man ogled her breasts? Would it excite him? Married twenty years and she can't even imagine.

By the time Lena gets there, the staff lot is full, pickups jammed in every direction, a plumber's van in her spot. She circles around to the visitor's lot and leaves her car under the bird shit tree. Inside, workers and patients mix together, clogging the works. Halfway down the hall she sees men removing tables and chairs from the nurse's lounge, Alice behind them stoked and smoking.

"What's going on here?" Lena catches up to them.

"I'll tell you what's going on here." Alice hands her a memo. "Your boy Strickland wants us to squeeze in more patients."

Lena reads it, balls it up and tosses it to a startled junkie.

"He in yet?"

"Been in. It's gung-ho honey."

"HEY! HEY YOU!" Lena barks at the flunkie with the coffee machine. "TAKE THAT AND I'M CALLING A COP!"

Three doors down Strickland mans the copy machine. There's a stool to the side, but he foregoes it in deference to the crease in his pants. The first new suit he's had in a decade, the girls in housekeeping checking him out. Strickland's the name, efficiency's the game.

And really, what could be easier? See which way the money goes, then make sure it doesn't get there. Wouldn't need a degree for that even if he had a stinking degree. Start with the perks, the drug rep lunches, the concurrent vacations, the endless overtime. Just revamping the schedule should save a bundle. And when he gets himself mobilized, and the unit softened up, he'll axe the whole program and save the freaking day! Oh yeah, shitcan the lot of them. Christ, Walters will HAVE to give him the corner office with the-

"Oh Mr. Strickland?"

"What is it Nurse Watts?"

"I'm just curious." Lena takes the seat by the copy machine. "When you decided to go ahead with these renovations, how did you think I'd react? I mean, considering my reputation and all."

Strickland busies himself with memos, a stapler, anything. "Quite frankly, I didn't take your reaction into consideration."

Lena fingers the hem of her skirt. "Do you think that was wise? See, ever since I was little, I've had this problem with my temper. You just wouldn't believe the trouble it gets me into. And it's not the kind of temper where you blow up and then forget about it."

"Nurse Watts I'm extremely bus-"

"It's the kind where you gotta get even. It's all about revenge with me, Strickland. You know, spreading rumors, plotting behind your back, stuff that makes for ... well, inefficiency."

"Come to the point, Nurse Watts."

"The point is this." Lena lets a shoe dangle. "If the nurse's lounge isn't turned back into the nurse's lounge by the end of the shift, the name Strickland shoots straight to the top of my shit list."

Strickland switches to his smarmy smile. "This is an administrative decision. It's nothing personal. The unit needs a higher census to remain viable."

"Save it, suck up. I've got that crap coming out of my ears."

"That doesn't change the fact. The hospital must have a solid plan of operation. It's my job to implement that plan. End of discussion."

"Oh, and the staff and I think it would be nice to have one of those cappuccino machines in the lounge, with the espresso maker?"

"Nurse Watts! I don't think you're behaving professionally. You'll find I don't respond well to threats and intimidation. I can assure you, the lounge will be restored when additional space is made available. Until that time, you will take your breaks in the cafeteria."

"By the board room?"

"The main cafeteria. It will do you good to mingle with the other staff members. Might relieve that detox mentality."

Lena studies her nails. "You know Strickland, a career is a funny thing. One miscalculation, a couple of bad decisions, and you find yourself being passed over."

Strickland pivots to the window and heaves a sigh. "More threats I see."

"Look at it this way." Lena reaches for the keys on his desk. "Alice and Dot have been here fifteen years. I've been here for six. You know how many pencil pushers we've been through?"

"That will be all, Nurse Watts."

"You might want to reconsider," she slips the keys in her pocket.

Strickland snorts. "Not a chance."

The kind of temper that sends her steaming out the front door, west on Tasker and up to the first broke down piper she sees. Not far, maybe three blocks as the bus flies.

"Julio, listen to me. … JULIO!"

"Hey Nurse Watts, what are you doing out here?"

She dangles a set of car keys in his face. "THIS is for the midnight blue Beemer in the executive lot. Think you can handle it?"

"Handle what?"

"Yes or no … OK, where's Manny? MANNY!"

"No hey," Julio snatches the keys. "I can handle it. Got a guard in the big wig lot though."

"I'll take care of Marvin. Just give me ten minutes."

"So, what do I get out of it?"

Lena drops the keys in his hand "I don't want to know anything. We never had this conversation."

Julio's rheumy eyes light up. "For real?"

"Don't screw it up, Julio." Lena starts back the way she came.

"What's going on? You OK over there?"

Lena turns and looks at him funny. "I'm sorry, do I know you?"

Julio grins and pockets the keys. "My mistake, I thought you was somebody else."

The door has a new nameplate. Henry Walters, Esq., Corporate Executive Officer in brushed brass framed by old screw holes. Lena shoulders her way inside, balancing med cups in either hand. A pair of manics trail behind, whining at each other. Walters springs from his desk, while Strickland sits scowling.

"Can we make this quick, fellas?" Lena skirts the desk and nods the whiners inside. "We're short downstairs, and all hell's breaking loose."

"Mrs. Watts, what is the meaning of this?" Walters stammers.

"Not to worry. They're with me."

"But why are they with you?"

"Well, I know how these head-butting sessions can run on and I figured I'd get some work done."

Walters marches to the door and summons his minions.

"Mrs. Worthman, would you please see that these patients are returned to the detox unit."

Firm but polite, just like in the book. By God he'll take care of this. Firm but polite, that's the ticket. Walters returns to his desk and motions Lena to take a seat. Lena hesitates for a moment, then hands the med cups to Strickland. Strickland scowls and sets them on the windowsill.

Walters begins. "Mrs. Watts, I'm going to ask you a simple question. I want you to answer 'yes' or 'no'."

"Gotcha."

"Do you know the whereabouts of Mr. Strickland's car?"

"I don't, sorry."

"Mr. Strickland has informed me that you've been harassing him with blackmail and threats of violence."

"I wouldn't call it harassing. Just laying some ground rules."

Strickland fidgets. Walters shoots him a look.

"Are you saying Mr. Strickland made it all up?"

"Sounds like it."

Walters conjures the book's cover, the jaunty corporate raider with the chainsaw.

"I see. You're suggesting that Mr. Strickland fabricated these threats, then stole his own car to discredit you."

"Brilliant, when you think about it."

"Have you been feeling all right, Mrs. Watts?" Walters tries another tack. Chapter Six, Changing Tack.

"Oh, I'm a little tired, what with the skeleton crew and inflated census. But, other than that …"

"Mrs. Watts, what would you say if I told you that you were seen driving off in Mr. Strickland's car yesterday afternoon?"

"I'll see you in court." Lena calls his bluff.

"I beg your pardon?"

"Watts vs. General Hospital and the Metro Medical Group, defamation of character, slander, pain and suffering."

"It's no secret you disapprove of Mr. Strickland's appointment."

"Your choice of words."

"We are talking about a crime here! A legal and moral outrage! How petty professional differences could come to this is incomprehensible to me." Walters slams the desk. Well placed outburst, Chapter-

"I'm calling my lawyer."

Walters wilts. "Mrs. Watts, please. Just between the three of us, what are the chances Mr. Strickland's car turns up this afternoon? No questions asked."

Lena frowns. "I'd say not good. It's chop shop city around here and the addicts know them all."

Walters wracks his brain for a chapter, but there's nothing in the book to cover grand theft auto.

"You're forcing me into a very awkward situation. You realize that, don't you?"

Lena puts on her poker face.

"We're talking about a felony here. A serious crime you're unwilling to rectify."

Nothing.

"Here's what I intend to do. As a last resort, I'm going to leave the room for a minute, in hopes that matters may still be resolved, in private, between two rational human beings."

"I wish you wouldn't," Strickland protests.

"Strickland, please." Walters holds up his hand. "Nurse Watts is a reasonable person. I firmly believe this. I'm sure if you impress upon her your intentions not to pursue the matter, not to seek recourse, as the case may be, two clear thinking professionals should be able to come to a mutually agreeable solution. Mrs. Watts? I trust this is possible?"

"Never say never."

Walters hesitates, then walks to the door, so quietly they can hear the brush of carpet. He turns once on the way out, then the door clicks closed behind him. Strickland eyes Lena. Lena pokes at a cuticle.

"That business in my office … you're a clever woman."

"That was nothing. Believe me."

"But you must be aware that, regardless of the outcome, your intentions have been revealed. Any further attempts to harass me would appear rather transparent, wouldn't you say?"

"Piss off, Bozo."

Strickland leans his elbows on his knees. "Might I remind you that in the chain of command, I am still your direct superior. Think about it, Nurse Watts. I'm in a position to make things rather difficult for you."

"You're history, pocket pal."

"I want my car back, bitch!"

Lena leaps up like she suddenly remembered something, the med cups, which she suddenly remembers to dump in Strickland's lap. Next thing he knows she's screaming bloody murder.

"PLEASE! MR. STRICKLAND, DON'T!"

Walters charges in as she's screwing herself into a corner bookshelf.

"HE SAID HE'D GET ME! THEN HE DUMPED THOSE MEDS ON HIMSELF!" She claws at a volume.

"That's a lie!" Strickland looks stricken. "I demand she be fired."

"KEEP HIM AWAY FROM ME! HE'S UNBALANCED!"

Strickland storms past Walters, who makes no move to stop him. The minions recoil at the trail of expletives down the hall. When there is nothing left to hear, Walters turns back to the room, and slowly closes the door. The minions huddle Like there's a madman in their midst.

"Sarah Jane? Miss Worthman? Could you excuse us for a moment?" Walters nods them out. He turns back, fusses with his volumes, then stares out the window at the swayback roofs of Pennsport. Lena smells a deal in the works.

"Now see here, Nurse Watts." She can't believe he'd start with that. "This is a disgraceful turn of events.

"Shocking, sir."

"Absolutely intolerable."

"I see you going far here, sir."

Walters pounds his fist on the desk, then struggles to compose himself.

"In a way, I suppose it's a good thing."

"How's that, Henry?"

"It makes it easier for me to make the decision," Walters shows his one true color, "to terminate the detox unit."

Lena rocks back half a step.

"Well," the smirky bastard smirks. "It appears we've hit a nerve."

"The whole unit?"

"Efforts are being made to place the others."

"Alice Long is fifty-two years old. Where are you going to place her?"

"These are uncertain times, Nurse Watts. If it's any consolation, it was only a matter of when. The unit was living on borrowed time."

"Borrowed time."

"Exactly. A simple matter of economics. The board had penciled you out even before the acquisition. It was only through my intercession that you shouldered on this long."

"Save it, Henry. How long do I have?"

"I'm afraid your termination is effective immediately. But you can close out the week without incident, I trust. Oh, and I wouldn't bother about filing a grievance. By the time the lawyers get through with it, there won't be a unit to return to."

"I'll be gone by tomorrow."

"If you prefer."

"What about Strickland?"

Walters smile is an orthodontic marvel. "Strickland's history."

Lena brings in muffins for the occasion. Raspberry and raisin for the crew, Ex-Lax marked with toothpicks for the undesirables. She knows it's childish, but that's the kind of girl she is. Dosing Walters would be long shot luck, but Strickland is a freeloading favorite.

They gather at break. She makes it official, and the crew howls in protest. Staff wanders in from ER and cardiac, and everyone rails against the injustice. But soon, it winds down to chin up and hang in there, the sad chant of the chronically clobbered. People she doesn't know drop around, doctors to dishwashers, Haitians from housekeeping, half the loonies in the bin. If there's a better grapevine Lena's never seen it. Word up on the toothpicks and no one goes near them.

"Aw hey, don't cry girlfriend." Lena hugs Alice tight.

"I ain't cryin'," Alice slobbers. "Must be these damn allergies."

"Come on, it's not like you'll never see me again."

"Yes, it is. That's just what it's like."

"But we go shopping every week!"

"Ain't the same." Alice turns away. "I know you from a thousand shifts. This is the Lena I know, right here."

A sad affair with the usual bluster, the yet to be compromised counseling the soon to be displaced. Heart wrenching but comical, with cops and claims adjusters taking statements in the lobby, the stolen Beemer a side item. Not that they had anything on Lena, hot cars in Crackville being as likely to resurface as the Phillies in late September. Her six years counting all the way down. When it's over, Lena clears out her desk and hands in her keys. Dot and Alice see her to her car, clutching at each other like the church girls they are. Halfway home, Lena spots Julio on the corner, poking a pager and dripping bling. She glances over once but he looks right through her.

SOLE SURVIVOR

I come around to the slap of salt water and a sea level view of nothing but blue. The boat, the Ballesteros, the Brandy Alexanders, gone. All of it. Lone survivor spared for worse. The smart money would have been on Ballesteros, all that brawn and blather, but BB's gone, and gone means dead. Her too, though it's hard to believe it. She was telling me something when we hit the reef, a loud crack and we both pitched forward. That's all.

Two dead, one yet to die.

Alone in the purest sense.

Only one thing to do, so I do it: pick a direction and start swimming. Lose the shoes, lose the pants, don't think, just focus. But even on its last track the mind feeds back images, the final flailing, the tortured breath, the drowned man's surrender to stillness. I've read the books, the people who survive against all odds. I know what it takes, and I don't have it.

But for now, swim. Toward or away from, no marking progress, no gap to close. What's left is to stop swimming, and that time will come.

Regrets. Aw, Jesus. Vienna for New Year's, a dream turned to dust even as I dream it. To see Angie again, if just for a moment, last time drunk with love and limoncello. The old demons raring up: my dog, my dad, my chosen path. What you don't miss until it's gone, a stiff drink and a chance to redeem yourself.

The life vest was no safety measure. I wore it for bulk, to fill space as BB did. I liked the way it looked, vanity as a survival skill. How I won't wear a seatbelt for fear of a wrinkle.

"I will not die," I say, to test the effect, a human voice, if only my own.

Then, on impulse.

"I will not say anything stupid."

The shoulders will go soon enough, then stomach and thighs from treading water, taking longer to rest. Good shape for my age, but not long for this shit. Cold now, and getting colder, maybe it's give up time before things get worse, muscle cramps, sharks and whatnot. Die in daylight, the little left of it.

Fuck me.

BB was a dick. The ocean always spooked me. She was the reason. Not to love, but to even the score, put the horns on BB as he did me. Late one night over too much wine, she told me the tale of Dr. Sardonicus. Her voice gave me pleasure, nothing more.

I stop to rest but there is no rest, straining for the surface, huffing in ragged gasps. Oh shit. Fucking shit. My Art Tatum records, the new bag of weed, oh sweet Jesus. My time ticking down in a groan of sorrow, wracked with grief, missing myself. Bye Mom … bye …

My eyes squeeze shut, but it's there when I look, a pale light ahead. And it's real all right, but I'll never reach it.

Kill me, God, only don't make me laugh.

I know now that rage saved those never say die boys. Nothing else can push us that far, no other force will prevail beyond pain to a zone of madness. Sink your teeth in the hand of fate, kill what would see you die, and even that's not enough. Luck draws last, so you have it or you don't, the way of the world, nothing personal.

I'm not thinking this. I'm not thinking anything. The light shines low on the water, lost to the swells, then there again. Choking now every few minutes, the vest straps rubbing raw. Can't move but can't sink either. Turned around in the tug of tide, then back again, and the light looks closer. I watch, then don't watch, could be the charm, too cold to function, too weak to form intent.

Closer still.

I end up curled into a sand dune, barely breathing and better off dead. First and worst of the castaway's fears; live through it to die anyway. Crazy with thirst, I stagger into the bushes, naked, shoeless, both feet bloody in twenty yards. Back to my dune, as if to get something, cell phone, shoes, my dune, as if I could find it. Cross the beach at a wobble, downwind and into the sun. Water somewhere, but how to find it? Fast.

Desert island, right?

Inland slopes uphill. Water runs down. Keep walking, my one shot and the most I can manage. Sure enough, it's not even far. A freaking lagoon and it's wade right in, drink my fill, soak up strength and chase down my senses. The squeal of gulls like nothing's amiss, a rush traced to a waterfall, picture perfect and me with no camera. A laugh like I've got this knocked, buck naked and ranting like a fool.

Immediate need duly met. I won't die of thirst, which is no great shakes, but gives weight to the moment. First bullet dodged. One-nothing, me.

The rest is academic with no shoes. Mid-afternoon by the sun, four hours of light left, maybe less. Food is top priority, or is it shelter? No clouds as of yet, but this is the tropics. Face the night wet or hungry? Probably both if I don't think of something. Wrapping my feet in leaves? Some guys, maybe, but not me in a million years. What then? Sit here when I can still move? Skirt the island, if nothing else. Keep to the sand, maybe stumble on something, a cave or culvert, an all night bodega. My snicker dissolves in waves of despair.

Now it's getting dark and I haven't done anything. Walked a little, dozed on a rock. Fuck it, I'm not up for this. Rain on the far horizon. Let it come. Go mad. Think candy bars, taco chips, beer pretzels crusted in salt. Think burgers and baked potatoes. Think of …

… the light!

Lost in the long day's coming to terms. The light was real. Someone's here.

I scan the hillside but there's nothing, a darker hump in the darkness. Do they know I'm here? You could hardly miss me all day naked on the beach. Either they're coming or they're hiding. If they're coming, it may be to kill me. If they're hiding, it may be to kill me. If they meant to save me, they'd be here by now, but they choose to wait. Or they didn't see me, or something's blocking the light. A cliff or an overhang, a bad angle, or maybe I'm too close. Or maybe there wasn't any light, just to cover everything.

If someone's here, they must have food. I think of Catherine Street, the pepper and egg sandwich I'd get on my way to work. I made a point to commit it to memory, and there it is. I could use a shirt now that the breeze has picked up. Shoes, of course, and anything you can think of, really. The correct time. A freaking match. What I need is help. What I don't need is a psycho in the bushes.

If someone were here they'd leave footprints. Tomorrow I will circle the island, or as much of it as I can, find a way to get myself out of this. Of course, that will mean leaving my footprints all over, but it can't be helped.

I sleep buried in the sand with a club in my hand.

So hungry it makes me nauseous, hollow inside, my stomach busy digesting itself. I eat some grass, just to see, ground up into shards, maybe a molecule of nourishment. I trap a bug but can't eat it, not alive. So, I smash it and forget about it.

But I can stand up. And except for a million bruises and scabs on my feet, I'm all right. What I know from the binge years I can go three days without eating a thing. Day Two the same as Day One weatherwise, my only break, but nothing to scoff at. So then, off I go and I'm OK, almost upbeat.

But my feet can't take it, and I stall in the shade, and stare morosely out to sea. My tan parts bronzed, the rest cherry red, lunchtime by the clock in my stomach, roast pork sandwich on the brain, ballpark franks, T-bone, thick and smothered in onions. Or a banana. I read somewhere you can sustain life on bananas. Not much of a plug, but something you remember when you have no bananas. Or coconuts, the other staple my desert island doesn't feature. Spear a fish. Think Tom Hanks in Castaway, except he was alone. Think violent death when I least expect it, which won't be any time soon.

That night I see the light. Midway up the hill, a fire looks like, maybe a mile off. Someone's up there doing God knows what. A fellow survivor, or something else entirely? I try to think what to do, but just go in circles. Crazy to try anything in the dark, but crazier to wait, and I'm fucking starved, so I go.

And it's agony, feet sliced to ribbons, but making a dent and stoking myself. Fuck it, do what it takes, let adrenaline kick in. It's daybreak when I reach the ledge. I follow the smoke to a guy hunched at a campfire, big guy in a trance of some sort. He's bearded and bald with a blue kerchief headband. Not much of a campsite. Roasting spit, stacks of wood, a bed of grass tucked in the rocks. Hasn't been here long, from the look of it. Clothes in fair shape, and he's wearing shoes. The fire dwindles, a mist settles over. I watch through the leaves but he doesn't move.

Then he does, rocking slowly side to side, drunk maybe, who knows? Then he's singing, softly at first then louder, the tune lost to volume, no language I've ever heard. Then he's quiet again, stone still, sensing my presence or sound asleep. Either way I stay where I am.

No food that I can see.

While getting here seemed so urgent, what to do is not so clear. Is he crazy? No way do I stroll out of the jungle and chum up a great big crazy man. And you would go crazy here if you didn't starve first. He comes across wacko. To me, crouched naked in the woods. Glued to the spot no less, thinking what would BB do? Ex-marine by way of a washout, windbag by trade, BB always had a plan. Half-baked to lame-brained, but a course of action, a move to make. I need some of that.

This guy's story … whatever it is, he brought stuff with him. The blanket strung on a line, for one. The line for another. That box by the bed didn't wash up on the beach. He had a boat. Or someone left him here.

And this trance and the singing, maybe it's a cultural thing, or a rescue rite, or just a guy by himself blowing off steam. Who doesn't act the fool when there's no one to see? No way for me to know, so I just watch. Him. The box. I just know there's food in it. Twinkies and Mars bars, chips and dip, I don't care. Head cheese, Tic Tacs, anything.

Who would leave him here, and why? Some score settled. He did something, killed somebody, or worse. A maniac with survival skills, and shoes, and that box of burgers. What else could explain him being here? My only hope is he'll go someplace so I can find the food. But where would he go? And what if he doesn't? Hunger will soon force my hand. How I can't imagine.

It gets worse. He spends an hour throwing a knife at a tree, and not missing once. Big, nasty knife, and the last thing I want to see. I'm so exhausted that I close my eyes for what feels like seconds, but when I look up in panic, he's gone! Did I fall asleep? Is he sneaking up behind me? I don't even breathe but the surf blocks the silence. I feel around for a rock, anything.

But then he's back again with three squirrels by the tail and I don't have to guess how he came by them. I watch him work the knife then fit the critters to the spit, and it takes a while, but the first whiff brings me to my knees. Meat sizzles not ten yards away, and I hug my knees, squeeze as hard as I can. What to do? What? But with his knife and my footprints, the conclusion is foregone. This place isn't big enough for two sole survivors.

He works the spit, and I creep in inches, centimeters. Do it while he's distracted. Kill him with this rock. Don't waffle. My only chance. He's got a weapon and a hundred pounds on me. And he will kill me, if only not to worry. My mind goes blank. I leap from behind and cave his head in.

Two years now, would be my guess, and not a day goes by where I don't miss him. American, from Ohio. There were letters, a book of crossword puzzles, but nothing to say why he was here.

His name was Stevenson. I knew a guy named Stevenson once.

STICKMAN

The guy at the door doesn't look like Danny, though a case could be made for the nose. A mashed in version, dramatically scabbed and weather beaten, and the hair, filthy but spiked in defiance. A strange, Dan-like head on a body that would make an anorexic flinch. Withered limbs swimming in cutoffs and stained polo shirt, Dead-end Danny after the rock fight. It couldn't be, yet the voice assures us it is, the South Philly accent unmistakable.

"What have you done to the real Danny?" my wife demands.

"C'mon Andree, let me in."

It was little more than a year ago, during the last dismal round in his squabble with the hospital administration that we saw him last. Bloodied but unbowed, he vowed to fight them to the end. Master of the cat and mouse game of drug counseling, Danny was as close to a legend as anyone in that line is likely to get. Confrontational, abrasive, and streetwise to a fault, he did what he had to do to reach the reachable. The bureaucrats were another story. The end was never really in doubt.

Now he's sitting in my kitchen, eating Fruit Loops, and making phone calls. The calls are brief. No one wants to hear from Danny these days. We'd heard rumors, but nothing could have prepared us for the wreckage. I console myself with a single thought. Originally, he was Andree's friend.

"I won't give you money," she sets the limit.

"Two bucks? Two bucks and I'm outa here."

"I'm a nurse. I can't give you money to cop."

Strange, after all these years, to hear her talk the talk again. He turns to me.

"Tom?"

"Jesus, what can you get for two bucks?"

He smiles. By God, it IS Danny.

"Where's Libby and the kids?" Andree asks. Again, he smiles.

Somewhere in the depths of her secretary desk is an in-house magazine with a faintly sneering Danny on the cover. Pre-crash and burn addict-savant in a black leather jacket. In the archives of the very hospital that fired him is a Dan-directed recovery video that leaves the unaddicted feeling strangely lacking. What have we to overcome?

"Where's little Danny?" Andree grills him. He mumbles something unintelligible.

It is her job to disapprove. Dazzled as I am by the plunge, the physical devastation, the ridiculous polo shirt, I try not to stare. It occurs to me that the bulk of the homeless once had a home, a bathroom and a closet full of clothes. This will not always be the case. The next generation is fast upon us.

He pours a small mountain of sugar on his Fruit Loops and we watch as it dissolves. The tattoos have not fared well, the dagger on his bicep reduced to a hatpin, the naked lady shriveled to a smudge. But it's the shirt that gets me. In real life, Danny would not own such a thing.

Andree plays the nurse/interrogator to Danny's strung-out supplicant. They speak in code, a mix of medicalese and doper slang. All the while, Danny smokes my cigarettes and shovels in the cereal. It's a toe-to-toe performance, masters of the genre, Andree projecting tough love with a no bullshit bottom line, Danny, in a perfect blend of psychic pain and sardonic wit. I sit fiddling with my fingers, in the loop, but out of my league.

"You want something else to eat?" I ask him. "A sandwich maybe?"

"No way, Jose. This guy gave me a sausage sandwich yesterday," he clutches at what's left of his stomach. "Tried to kill me, I tell ya. I said later for you, Mr. Sausage."

Danny has a jargon all his own, Port Richmond patois laced with goofy names and words you have to look up

"I got some green chile salsa," I make a joke. They roll their eyes and tune me out. Different treatment centers are suggested and rejected. Andree persists, Danny resists. References to HIV are impossibly oblique, pauses mostly, a hardening of the eye. It's a pointless exchange when you stop and think. Danny invented the game. If anyone knows where the treatment centers are, it's him.

I slip him three bucks under the table.

"You need a ride somewhere?"

He reaches past me and steals another cigarette.

"Florida," he gives a wink. "Winter's coming, don't you know."

For the next hour Andree works the phone, calling in a decade's worth of markers. The old girl network of admission nurses finds a place for him in the Benton Institute, though he has no medical card or even valid ID. During the negotiations Danny tells me about the car he shares with a friend on the west side.

"Well at least you can get around." I put my clueless spin on things. His look says, *later for you Mr. Andree.*

He was clean for seven years. Worked a job, got married, bought a house and had kids. Amazing what you can do in seven years. At the reception for his son's christening, he commandeered the stage to serenade his bride. There wasn't a dry eye in the house. Neighborhoods. Where you can still be a hero, or even worse.

A week later we go to see him. Benton Institute, with its pillared porches and fairway grounds, looks more Main Line then medicinal, its present function as unlikely as its location. Walled off from surrounding badlands, a fair share of the city's pipers could walk there in minutes. We meet him at the med station, still wasted, but showered and shaved. The only patient we'll see who looks like a patient.

"They're cutting me down to 40 milligrams a day," he complains as he leads us down lavish hallways to his room. "I mean, what ever happened to coddling?"

"You're here to get well, not to get high." Andree toes the line. As usual, my presence is not required. I trail behind them, scanning the paintings and Queen Anne furniture.

"Nice place," I tell him.

"Oh yeah, it's like drying out in Graceland."

His is a corner suite with a view of the rose garden. Two single beds and a chest of drawers. Fireplace. Despite our protests, he insists on showing us his feet, which have suffered some withdrawal related malady too gruesome to get into. My own toes curl in sympathy. Andree turns away.

"Will they get better?" I ask him.

Danny shrugs and wiggles the big ones at me.

"Will we?" the right one wonders in falsetto.

"Beats me," the left one bows from the waist.

He doesn't last long at the Institute. A late-night phone call confirms Danny checked out against medical advice. The news comes as no surprise, and whatever comes next will not include us. And I'm thinking, clawing your way back should be enough. Do the right thing, and the right things should happen. But addiction rigs it different. When the game is never over, how can you win?

You don't hear much about crackheads these days, but that's just because we got tired of listening. Too much worry and troubles of our own. In the meantime, they're out there hitting rock bottom. The scufflers, the sidewalk sleepers, the stickman who used to be Danny.

THE REAL THING

It was always autumn when Charlie Sikes emptied the machines at North Shore. He could still recall that first year, driving the lake road through flaming trees, listening to the World Series on the radio, the sun warm on his left arm and Drysdale setting them down in order. Some men would envy him, he remembered thinking.

A lot had changed in forty years. They played the Series at night, now, for one. For another, the resort they'd planned for North Shore never really panned out. The ski lift and lodge hung on a few years, but the real skiing was two hours further north, where the resorts knew how to play the game. It seemed to Charlie that the effort to change had taken a toll on North Shore. More places went broke than broke even, and the locals had the hangdog look of the snookered. Too bad for them, Charlie snorted. A year from now he'd be in Tampa and North Shore would be someone else's problem.

One more year. The blink of an eye.

The machine at Pike's Chicken Shack was of the new style: weatherproof, graffiti proof, lots of jazzy colors. He'd brought it up himself two summers ago to replace the round-shouldered box that had been there since God knows when. Pike's hadn't changed much, still family-style, still socking enough away each summer to shut down after Labor Day. When old Pike died, his kids made a go at year-round, but the hunters and the truckers proved more trouble than they were worth. Pulling into the gravel lot, Charlie could see that the awnings had been taken down and the windows shuttered.

It only took a minute. He unplugged the machine, taped the coin slot, and loaded the bottles onto the truck. Mindful of the moment, Charlie took in the breeze and the rustle of leaves. Not likely he'd be up this way again soon. So intent was he on marking the occasion, he didn't see the cat slink around the corner, poke his nose along the open Coke machine door, then slip inside. Had anyone been watching, they might have called out, maybe shared in a laugh at a cat's lack of sense. But no one was watching, no one called, and Charlie shut the door with a resounding thunk.

"Well," he said out aloud, feeling slightly foolish. "I guess that about does it."

He stepped up into the cab and filled out the inventory report. He suddenly recalled that that long ago game that Drysdale won. He'd listened to the last out right here in this parking lot, joking with the Pikes, and sneaking a beer in celebration. Hadn't given it a thought since the day it happened. How many guys put in forty years humping a delivery truck? Not too many, he suspected.

Paperwork finished, Charlie lit the cigar he'd saved for the occasion and took a long last look around. It was still pretty country up here, but too far for commuters and not far enough for a weekend toot.

"Luck of the draw," Charlie whispered to himself, then circled the lot and took off down the road. Two kids trailed after him on bikes. A stone truck thundered past. A pair of crows swooped and squabbled.

Inside the Coke machine, the young cat crouched in the delivery chute. The door had stunned him and the mouse he'd been chasing was lost to the darkness. If he were human, he would have seen the hopelessness of his situation. With no way out, panic would have seized him. But he was a cat, and his thoughts were of the darkness, total and absolute. In the time it would take him to die or be rescued, his eyes would be of little use. Reduced to sound, and the smell of molded plastic, gear oil, the stone trucks, and the mice, the cat stood up, circled once, and sat staring. The darkness gave him nothing. He washed one arm and the back of an ear, then circled back and settled on his haunches. The wind signaled the change in seasons. His mind went blank, and he fell asleep.

The smell of water woke him and he sniffed out a puddle in the lip of the frame. He lapped away, then stretched as best he could. Turning around, he tried to force his head past the delivery flap, but the slot was too narrow. He reached a front leg between the chute and the door, but it wouldn't fit. He lapped at the water. Again, he tried to reach his leg through, but nothing had changed, so he slept.

Through the night, he alternately stretched, turned, fit his leg through the gap, and slept. He missed the nightly dollop of cat food and the table scraps the woman gave him, and the crumbs of TV snacks and puddles of ice cream at the bottom of the bowl. His was an easy life. He wanted for nothing and nothing was asked of him. Had he killed the mouse, he wouldn't have bothered to eat him.

He'd eat him now.

The cat's home was through the woods behind the Chicken Shack. He didn't come to Pike's for the garbage. He was a hunter, not a scavenger, though he made an exception on Crab Cake nights. He came for the mice, stalking, pouncing. The first time he saw one something clicked, his raison d'etre right there gnawing a French fry.

Mice were so easy, he sometimes signaled his presence or gave a head start. He liked when they hid beneath the Coke machine, the waiting game they couldn't win. Too frightened to freeze they'd make a mad dash. That's when he'd get 'em. Always he would get 'em … except this once.

By morning his stomach churned and he howled in frustration. The mouse he'd followed in had managed to escape. Leon could tell from the absence of smell. Most of the time it was quiet, if you can call birds in the morning, locust and stone trucks all day, tree frogs and crickets into the wee hours, quiet. He knew the cycle instinctively, but only the birds held any interest. He'd caught his share, but their wings were an advantage. If it was a young bird he was after, the others would gang up, and more than once he'd taken a hit. The blue jays were the worst with their screeching and dive-bombing. All things considered, he preferred mice.

"Leee – on! Here kitty-kitty. Here Leee – on!"

The cat yowled once then meowed pitifully. She'd named him Leon after a character in one of her children's books. The little girl loved Leon with all her heart. He loved her too, but what he missed most was the man of the house, football double headers, pizza and lunchmeat. The man would rub Leon's stomach obsessively, pausing only to hoot and holler. It wasn't affection, more like ritual and nerves, the closer the game, the more the man rubbed. His motivation didn't matter to Leon. Hoots and hollers were a small price to pay.

"Leee-on! Here boy!"

The calls came no closer. He whined a few times, but no one could hear. Soon the woman shouted something, and the calls stopped. Leon turned, stretched, and settled back down. Just before dusk, a sliver of sunlight seeped through a crack in the door seal. He rose up to give it a sniff. In less than a minute the light was gone.

When Leon had to pee he backed down the chute to give it some distance. For three days he resisted moving his bowels, but he'd always been regular and on the fourth day, he relented. It was humiliating. With no litter or grass to cover his business, he did the only the thing he could. Rearing up, he braced himself and kicked it past the delivery flap.

Leon stopped grooming to conserve moisture. He spent his time sleeping, though positions were limited. Once, he dreamt the little girl was feeding him ice cream. His tongue rounded the bottom of the spoon, then shoveled it off the concave center--vanilla, his favorite. When he woke and realized he'd been fooled, he whined the night away.

At least he thought it was night. With no light except the brief sliver, he was fast losing track. He only knew it was high time to eat and drink. That was what he thought about when he wasn't sleeping. Not the pain of hunger, but the act of eating; not thirst, but the sound of the faucet running. The little girl turned it on for him every night while she brushed her teeth. She was very thorough about brushing, which gave Leon time to drink his fill.

The mice knew something was up. They hadn't seen the cat in days, yet he was still here, the smell and sound of him. Mice may be skittish, but they have to eat, and before long, a few ventured forth. Leon howled his presence, but when he didn't appear, the mice grew bolder. The old dumpster had been a mouse haven for generations, serving up a smorgasbord of scraps. Now and then a cat would raid, but never for long, and never like this one. This one never missed. They didn't know what he was doing in the box, but they soon figured out he couldn't touch them. In a matter of days the dumpster was teeming.

What sounded like heavy fingers tapping turned out to be rain. At first he thought the mice had gotten in, but the thunder rumbled and he knew what it was. All the same to Leon, something new to listen to, so he listened to it. Before long, the lip of frame filled with water and he drank to his heart's content. To the extent a cat can ruminate, the rain made things interesting. He knew the mice were still out there. A little rain wouldn't put them off. When the wind kicked up, he could hear the leaves rattle and the old pines groan in the distance. Farther still, a fawn was bleating, and beyond that, he could hear the creek. After a while the mice gave it up, the fawn fell silent, the wind died down, and he was left with the rain.

Since mice have to eat, they'll search out anything to find food, even a tiny crack in the Coke machine's frame. Leon could smell the foolish little mouse and the mouse could smell Leon. Getting in wasn't hard, but getting out in the dark in a panic proved too much for him. Trapped and terrified, the mouse simply died of fright, and after a bit of a struggle to reach him, Leon ate the poor thing, bones and all. A week later it happened again. Among mice, word spread of the missing, and thereafter they stayed away.

Every so often someone stopped for a Coke. Leon tried to cry out, but his croak would not project and the tape over the coin slot soon sent them on their way.

Shortly after Halloween, the weather turned cold. By then, Leon's muscles were withered and when he turned, which was seldom, he was frail and unsteady. His fur was greasy and his breath sour. He slept entire days away and didn't move his bowels for weeks at a time. Hunger no longer hounded him, only the cold. Positions were limited to a tight curl on his left or right side with his paws tucked and head curled under. Awake, his mind clouded with misery.

The cold held on into November, and a week before Thanksgiving it snowed a foot. Snowplows used the lot for dispatch.

Motors rumbled, men milled about in the brittle morning light. Leon heard none of it. By now, his life signs were dim, and his breathing intermittent. But Leon wasn't dead. He'd lost all contact with the living world, but he was still a part of it.

Life in North Shore blundered on. Two days after Leon's senses shut down, Audrey Lane spotted her neighbor at the roadside mailbox on her way home from the supermarket. She pulled her car to the shoulder to share a bit of gossip, but misjudged the distance and ran her right over. The rumor spread that Audrey had a drinking problem, and in her remorse, the rumor came true.

A week later a flatbed trailer backed into a job site and made off with the county's new grader. Police rounded up the usual suspects, but the culprit came from out of state, and the grader was never recovered. The rumor that the chief of police was involved eventually cost him his bid for reelection.

Over at North Shore High, a new boy pulled a knife on the school bully and threatened to "cut his balls off." The new boy was sent to the juvenile center, but returned in a month to a hero's welcome. The bully's father filed a lawsuit, but a dozen kids testified to their torment and the case was dismissed.

Just a stone's throw away from the Chicken Shack, a little girl awoke on her birthday to find a kitten wrestling with one of her slippers. She was a sentimental girl and in memory of her first pet, she named the kitten Leon.

The rains returned soon after Christmas. For weeks the skies ran steely grey. Temperatures hovered just above freezing and the storms turned the North Shore lawns to lagoons.

Basements flooded, roofs leaked, and housebound children drove their folks crazy. No one could remember a winter so wet. Inside the Coke machine, water pooled on the coin box housing. More than enough to quench any cat's thirst, but Leon was lost in a dreamless void. In his suspended state, Leon registered nothing. But the spark of life still flickered, and every now and then an ear would twitch or a muscle quiver. As the weeks turned to months, his fur grew thicker and his claws curled over his toes. Any colder and he would have frozen, but the winter wore on as the warmest on record.

Most people would think it impossible. Nothing living could survive such a thing. But the cat is a confounding creature, and the myth of nine lives has some basis in fact. In free fall, a cat's limbs will billow. They've been known to fall ten stories and walk away. A cat would never think to chase a car, or run into a burning building. Unless it's old, sick, or badly injured, a cat doesn't know how to die.

So Leon held on by a thread. Christmas came and went and the old year passed into the new. By mid-January, the girls' basketball team was the hot topic, and further north, ski lift operators cursed the snowless skies. Across the woods, the little girl tired of her kitten's bad behavior and banished him to sleep in the garage. She often pined for *her* Leon, but only the mice knew what had become of him.

Then, one night, for reasons undetermined, the Chicken Shack gas line sprang a leak. And lacking Pike Senior's attention to detail, Junior had left a pilot light on. The blast lit up the North Shore sky, and blew the Coke machine across the parking lot. The place was an inferno when the fire trucks got there, so they shut down the road and let it burn. In the smoking haze of daybreak, a pair of firemen sat on the toppled Coke machine. The younger one thought he heard a sound from inside. They listened for a moment, then took a crowbar to it. Leon curled away from the light.

"Well, I'll be damned." The older man shook his head in wonder. "How do you suppose he got in there?"

"Probably kids." The young one ran a hand over Leon's ribs. "Hardly nothing left of him."

"This place has been closed up for months," said another. "You don't think he's been in there all that time, do you?"

"I wouldn't put nothing past a cat," the older man cackled. "My sister had one disappeared for over a year. One night, she heard something at the back door, and when she opened it, there he was. Sumbitch had one eye missing and an ear chewed off, but other than that, he was good as new."

"Worthless goddamn animals," a fourth spit in disgust. "We ought to just toss him in the coals."

The older man rose to his feet. "You lay a hand on that cat and I'll toss *you* in the goddamn coals."

The young fireman lifted Leon out. His spine was bent and his legs were drawn up, but his ears still swiveled and they took this as a sign.

"It's okay, pal. We'll take care of you. You just rest and we'll have you back on your feet in no time."

And so they did. Someone brought a cat bed to the station. They covered Leon with blankets and watched over him like parents. At first he could only swallow broth, but as his strength returned, so did his appetite. Local cat lovers offered assistance and kids ran a fund drive to cover expenses. The vet pronounced Leon blind and malnourished, but his organs still functioned and his remaining senses were miraculously intact.

After heated debate, the men named him "Sparky." North Shore's mayor alerted the press and reporters covered the story. Overnight, "Sparky" was front-page news. Donations poured in along with offers of adoption, but the firemen claimed the cat as their own, and in a ceremony broadcast on the evening news, Sparky was named their official mascot.

Shortly after, the station house got another visitor. Flushed and breathless, the little girl pushed her way through, and at the sight of her Leon, she fell to pieces. The men were so touched, and the girl was so sweet, the whole town beamed at the happy ending.

Turned out, it was just the beginning. Within days, the pair was featured on *Good Morning North Shore,* and named grand marshals of the Memorial Day parade. Then the Internet got wind of it and by mid-summer the world knew Leon's story. Bloggers dubbed him the Coca-Cola Cat and his face graced the cover of *People Magazine*. The soft drink giant did their bit with a new fire truck and a scholarship fund for the little girl. In a summer of global tension and economic stress, a lost cat story was made to order.

But feel-good stories have a short shelf life. By summer's end the buzz played out and the cat resumed life as a normal, if sightless, household pet--which was fine with Leon. He didn't mind being blind, and had all but forgotten his four-month ordeal. Aside from a family ban on rearranging the furniture, his affliction had no lasting effects. In an effort to keep him from wandering off, the girl's dad fitted a tracking device to his collar. But the gizmo proved defective and Leon soon managed to slip away. His recall of his former life was spotty, but one thing he could never forget. Using traffic sounds to gauge distance, he kept to the shadows so the birds wouldn't see. Clearing the trees at a trot, he crossed the clearing to the parking lot. The site smelled of smoke, lumber, and paint from the Cola Cat Shack (Junior's bid to cash in). Leon stopped to think things through. He knew without seeing that the dumpster was gone. Moving closer, he sniffed along the network of nests and furrows, but there was no trace of mice. At the Shack, he checked the foundation, sorting through odors, none of them rodent. Then the smell of plastic struck a chord, and he bolted to the high ground. With the sun on his back and his face to the wind, Leon crouched and listened.

Before long a truck pulled in carrying Pike Junior with a ladder and a Grand Opening sign. Had he been human and not blind, Leon might have laughed at his Cola Cat likeness. But cats have a rarefied sense of humor and things like that don't strike them as funny.

Junior paced the length of the building, taking in his new sign from every angle. Then he sat in the car and looked at it some more. Leon closed his eyes and drifted in a doze, waking at the sound of Junior leaving. Seconds later a cloud settled over: exhaust, a bit of rot …

Leon's eyes snapped open and his ears swiveled right. Scanning scents, he tracked location, zeroed in and began to purr. The mouse would panic, nothing else left for it, just a matter of when and which way. Leon closed in slow, and slower still, a pause for the pounce, then head-first into Junior's new handicapped parking sign. More staggered than hurt, he circled off and faced the darkness, fixing their positions. The mouse was still there. Leon knew it, and the mouse knew he knew it. Down to this, the silence of time, deadly deep in the absence of man. The sun slipped behind a cloud. The mouse made his break. Leon stood, stretched and turned for home.

Who knows why the mouse was spared? The signpost may have stung more than Leon's nose, or maybe the Coke machine finally spooked him. More likely it was age, and who needs this anyway? Some might say it was compassion, but they'd be wrong. Cats know nothing of compassion.

SCORE

Snow rumbles against the floorboards, pushing me sideways. Flakes as big as doilies swirl into my headlights while the wipers do the best they can. They're calling for a foot in the outlying areas, and an outlying area is right where I'm headed, to Andree's disbelief and my own dismay. Tyrone's call came shortly before midnight. I rolled out of bed and summoned my strength.

"You're out of your friggin' mind," was how Andree put it.

"Come on, it's not that bad out." I struggled into my pants. "The weather guys always exaggerate."

"Fine. I'm unplugging the phone."

"You should be glad he called. You know how I get."

How I get is unbearable. Instead of the usual mood swings, I bottom out completely. Without weed, all the wheels stop turning, and I mope around heaving sighs of despair. Any task seems beyond me. I can't sleep and I have nothing to say. It's not like I take it out on Andree, but hey, she's there.

The snow's not so bad under the L if I keep to the inside lane. If I were stoned, I'd be thinking how unworldly this looks, the weird light, the iron canopy, the deserted streets and sidewalks. Crossing 41st Street, I steal a glance at the walled compound that was once the Tyler estate, is currently the Pennsylvania Institute, and will soon be something else, tucked away under snow-draped sycamores, a rich man's dream gone horribly wrong. If I were stoned it would strike me as funny. The world would look strange and magical, and the rattle in the heater wouldn't worry me a bit. I'd see the gas tank as one quarter full instead of three-quarters empty.

But I'm not stoned. Six days now without a buzz and the world is cold and ugly. Pretty much hitting a new low here, the notion that midnight was actually a good time to go to Tyrone's, the idea of beating the traffic and the snow removal crews turned delusional here in the thin vapor light. Laughable, even if I'm not laughing. What you lose sight of when you're fooling yourself is the odds against the street you need being cleared. I've passed one plow parked in a Wendy's lot, snow up to the fucking gunwales.

The el ends at 59th Street and I'm on my own, fishtailing along Cobb's Creek, then a wide left onto Haverford, plumes of snow in my wake. Traffic lights keep time in the absence of traffic. My nose is running and there's a knot of tension in my shoulder. The gas gauge is now halfway between the quarter mark and the big red E, where just blocks ago it was dead on a quarter. How is that possible?

Andree thinks I have a problem. She doesn't say anything, but it's in the air. She sees the weed as an extravagance, and she knows I'll never pass a drug test if I don't give it up. As if it was that easy. I tell her the test is unreliable, that employers use it as a ruse to filter out the faint of heart. Flunking three took the wind out of those sails, but it's not like you can skip a few joints and pee Perrier. It takes months without to clean the system and months is not an option. OK, I'm an addict, but it's not like I'm shooting smack and robbing people. Just reefer. No harm, no foul. I still eat right. I still bathe every day. The way Andree says nothing says it all. But silent disapproval is not what I need right now. Christ, you'd think I was pawning the silver.

Pothead. A failing, sure, but it's not like there's no upside. I'm a scream when I'm stoned. Ask anybody. Ask Tyrone. My impression of a cat coughing up fur balls always brings down the house. I'm not nearly as contrary when I'm high and I'm much smoother with the women. Plus, I can watch almost anything on television. Kicking pot might not kill me. I'd just wish I was dead.

Tyrone's snores carry through the storm windows and I see him sprawled on the couch with the TV going. I tap on the glass, but that'll never to do it. Tyrone is a world–class snoozer and nothing short of a referee's whistle is going to reach him. I could call from the phone booth, but then I'd wake Sharon, and the baby.

I tap again and the cat jumps up to sniff at my fingers. I rap harder with my knuckles and she does the shadowboxing thing. I can hear the snow falling behind me, a light hiss that deepens the silence. I picture it piling up on my lamppost at home, filling the lone set of tire tracks on Haverford.

On the off chance, I roll back the mat and what do you know? Now all I have to do is unlock the door and walk in.

Except when I picture it all kinds of things go wrong. You don't just walk into a guy's house in West Philly at one in the morning, even if he is expecting you, especially the house of a Black guy with a kilo of weed and paranoid tendencies. Just the kind of bonehead move you read about in the papers, under the photo with the crime scene tape. But if I don't do it, I'm back to square one. I fit the key in the lock and push the door open. Tyrone is sitting up, looking right at me.

"Dude," he flashes a sleepy smile.

"Hey." I walk in and toss him the key. "You might want to find a better hiding place."

"Duuuude, where you beeeen?"

"Sorry. The weather outside is frightful."

"I'm thinking my boy slipped up, wrapped his sorry ass around a pole. What's your old lady think about you dogsleddin' cross town to cop a bag?"

"She thinks I have a problem. What do you think?"

"I think even pipers stay home on a night like this! Sit down, Slim. You're looking peaky."

"Peaky?"

"Peaky."

"I can't stay long," I sink into the recliner.

"Why? What you gotta do, slacker?"

"I've got to maintain a semblance of routine. Daytime is for business. Nighttime is for TV and sleeping. This was all wrong, Tyrone. This …"

"Smacks of desperation?"

"Yeah, yeah, I guess so. Maybe desperation is a little strong."

"Now Tyrone?" He aims a finger at himself. "Tyrone don't go out that door until springtime. Not for nothing or nobody. I've made all the arrangements."

"What kind of arrangements?"

"Sharon goes to school and does the shopping. I watch the kids."

"What if something happens? The kids get sick? There's a gas leak?"

"If the kids gotta go somewhere, I call Aunt Serena. She owes me big time."

"Gas leak?"

"Dude, something like that and I'm outa here. OK? I'm not looking to go up in flames. I'm just, uh, uh, uh, setting a goal for myself."

"Of sorts."

"And, you know, I'm a goal-oriented motherfucker. I can do this. April."

"And I can say I knew the man. Knew him personally."

We smoke a bowl out of one of Tyrone's contraptions, a long, gunky tube with foul liquid bubbling at the bottom, and a finger hole on the side for those real bell ringers. The way that works, you toke a good three hits into the tube, then take your finger from the hole and whammo! Out of body experience.

"Between you and me, I'd go nuts staying inside all the time," I tell him. "With kids? I give you a month."

"Been TWO months already. First frost Tyrone was on it. Anyway, Angie's at St. Matthews, and Jeanette just started pre-school. Alarm goes off, they eat their Cheerios and book."

"What do you do all day?"

"Watch TV."

"How can you do that?"

He looks at me. "You mean how can I actively avoid doing something productive with my life? How can I fritter away the best years watching Yosemite Sam blow his own goddamn brains out?"

"In good conscience, I mean."

"You think Mr. White Man is gonna hire me? Get real, my brother."

"The race card."

"I heard that!"

Tyrone grew up in a white neighborhood, so he does his best to look the crackhead: glassy eyed, hair sticking up in clumps, big butt hanging out of his pants, and complicated sneakers right out of the box. His wife Sharon is a white girl from Ireland, if you can believe it. Red hair, freckles, about as far from the 'hood as you can get. Their two girls are angels, and every time I see them, I want to go home and have me some.

"I was tripping man," he says, telling me about a frat party he went to. Tyrone's less than half my age. "The bitch is heaving her guts out, and this other bitch is screaming about the rugs. Puking man, and it's got chunks and shit. And my boy's got his hands out and he's trying to catch it, you know?" Now he's laughing, a deep, phlegmy wheeze that's pure Tyrone. "But it's splashing down his arms, and between his fingers, and the look on his face? Buckwheat, yo!" He gives me the wide eyes.

"You call women bitches?"

"Say what?"

"I don't know, man. It's unbecoming."

"Naah, it's a Black thing. What we call uh, uh, uh, term of endearment."

"Bitches."

"And hoes."

We met when I was running presses at U of P. He was just out of high school, working in the bindery. It wasn't long before we were getting loaded at lunch and shit-canning the afternoon. Seems like a million years ago now.

On TV, the Keystone Cops are chasing crooks, legs going a mile a minute. They shake their fists, and make angry faces, and when they fall, they land on their keesters.

"Now this," Tyrone shoots a finger at the screen, "this shit is funny."

"Your best years."

"Look at those little white motherfuckers go!"

"Your momma's gonna chew your butt, Tyrone."

"Shiiiii-it," with a hint of uncertainty. Momma Henrietta, I happen to know, is the butt chewingest woman in West Philly. Another movie begins, the Keystone Cops in Dangerous Desperados. Somewhere along the line I lose contact with my legs.

"Got some Molson's on ice, Slim."

"No thanks, I gotta go."

We hear something in another room, a baby's whine stretching to a wail. Tyrone scrambles from the couch and darts down the hallway, returning moments later with Jeanette over his shoulder.

"S'OK baby, it's only the white man," he sidesteps past me. "Don't worry, Daddy won't let him oppress you."

She gives me a sleepy smile and wave.

"Hey kitten, you come to see me?"

She nods shyly then busies herself with Tyrone's buttons.

"Watch this, honey. Check it out." He points her at the TV. "This is important."

She stares at the men racing around in circles.

"See baby? Can you say Cau-casian?"

"Caw Cayjn," she giggles.

"I love my kids, man." Tyrone shoots me a wink. "Girl babies, ain't nothing bad about them."

"Caw Cayjin." She looks to me and points a dinky finger.

"That's my girl. Ain't you a trip? We have fun, don't we baby?" He turns her to him, then lifts her over his head and spins her like a propeller. Jeanette shrieks with laughter and he does it again. I'm no dad but I can see problems with this.

"Come on, sugar," he sets her down. "Show Slim what you can do. This is killer, man. I take her down to Barney's and drink all night for free."

"I thought you didn't go out."

"Daytime, dude. Tyrone's gotta have his social life. Come on, baby. Show the white man what you do."

She clasps her hands from behind. "I can say my ABC's."

"You can? Gee, that's -"

"In two seconds," Tyrone leans in.

Jeanette nods eagerly.

"Do the whole bit for him baby. Like we do it at Barney's."

She toddles over and pokes me on the knee. "Scuse me mister. Could I interest you in a little wager?"

"Sure sweetheart."

She takes a pretend something from her pocket and puts it on the arm of the recliner.

"A dollar says I can say my ABC's in two, count' em," she flashes fingers, "two seconds."

I place my own pretend dollar next to hers, but she shakes her head from side to side.

"That's not a dollar."

"What do you mean? That's a ten."

" … Oh."

"That's OK, baby," Tyrone nuzzles her ear. "Slim here is a chiseler. You remember what I told you?"

She bobs her head. "Chiselers burn in hell."

"Thaaat's right. Go on now. Show him."

Jeanette steps back, takes a deep breath and fixes her eyes on the wall behind me.

"ABCDelamentoZEE."

"HO now! Record time, baby, record time," Tyrone give her a squeeze. "Show him what else I taught you."

She reaches a hand under her top and makes little fart noises with her armpit.

Tyrone beams at me.

"Hey, I'm speechless!"

"She really picks things up quick. Don't you sweetie." More nuzzles and kisses. Aw jeez.

Halfway through The Keystone Cops in Moonshine Mayhem, the two of them are snoring away. I cover them up, show myself out and slip the key back under the mat.

It's not so bad going home. Still snowing but the plows have been out, at least on the main streets. I punch up the radio and fall into some Milt Jackson, just the thing for a stoned drive home, Philly Joe tapping rim shots, ba didlee dink a-dink a-deedee. Yeah, I know my jazz guys. Bags, Bird, Monk, Trane. I'm hip. City slick. Baggledee Beebop, got my dope, dope, dope. ...

So it went OK. Tyrone hooked me up, now I'm set for the month. Maybe a red flag or two in there, but nothing to beat myself up over.

But that's just what I do. Fifty-two years old and I'm dashing through the snow to feed a twenty-year habit. Hair going, teeth going, eyes going. Whoa boy, easy. Definitely not the buzz I need right now. I pull into Wendy's for coffee to go. A Penndot crew takes up half the counter, big guys with beards. I give one a nod but it sails right past him. Fuck you plowboy. Back in the car, I fish a roach from the ashtray and let 'er rip. Big hit, the usual hacking and histrionics, then another, then one more. I sit for a moment as the elements recombine, Sonny Rollins blowing, the wipers not quite hitting the beat. The rattle from the heater has stopped for the moment, and the cold air feels good through the open windows. I drink coffee until the reefer dissipates. Not even moving when I run out of gas.

THE LIP

When Julie left, she took half their stuff. Leo found a check-list and a note under her key ring on the counter. Even with Mario's help it must have taken most of the day. The note said she was leaving the car. He could make the payments or sell it, Julie's way of being more than fair. There were several points he would have contested, but Leo had to admit she'd been generous. All his wives had been generous. It was small consolation.

For days afterward Leo's life was like a dream. He thought about Julie and Mario driving across the country. In his head, they were always whooping it up. He wished them dead in the desert, their bodies black and bloated. The image so disturbed him he wished them back to life.

To take his mind off things, Leo went to the ball game. He brought his binoculars, a bag of salted peanuts, two joints and his Walkman. The right-hander, Rivera, was going for the Phillies. Big kid, clueless. Leo sat in one of the empty sections under the scoreboard. The binoculars gave him a bird's eye view of the strike zone. From the first pitch, Leo could tell the kid had it. Every fastball punched a dust-cloud from the catcher's mitt just before the clap of leather reached him in center field. The big lug got hammered early, but for two and a half hours, Leo didn't think of Julie once.

The following Sunday he drove to Rittenhouse Square and read the paper. The park was crowded, but no one approached him. Julie would be in San Francisco by now, badmouthing him to their west coast friends. Funny, none of them had called. He pictured the other half of their stuff in a North Beach apartment, sun streaming in the windows, Chronicle spread over the sofa.

That night Mario called. Julie had dumped him as soon as they hit the city.

"Swear to God, Leo, I never laid a hand on her," he insisted.

"What are you calling me for?"

"Hey man, I feel like a shit."

"You are a shit."

"I'm coming back, Leo. You can kill me if you want to, but I can't take it here."

"Come on back. I won't kill you."

"Oh man, I feel like such a shit."

Mario showed up on Friday. Despite his rejection, he looked much the same, half-drunk, pacing the kitchen berating himself.

"I mean, how could I do that to you?" He jabbed a finger in his own chest. "My best fucking friend! What the fuck is wrong with me?"

"You're a shit. You couldn't help it."

"You're right, Leo. You've always said it, but now I believe it."

"Believe it."

He stayed three days then left to mooch off a cousin. Mario was related to half the wops in South Philly. Leo'd never known him to have a place of his own. What did he expect to do in California?

On Easter Sunday, Leo walked to his mother's. As always, he was taken by the photos on the walls, chronologically arranged portraits, Leo and his sister Gail, Gail and her two kids, and one of his dad in a straw hat over the mantel. Gail divorced and moved to Florida two years ago, leaving Leo to deal with the obligations. The tone never varied.

"I don't understand my own children," his mother slipped a Camel from the pack on the table. "Your father and I were married forty-five years!"

"Thirty-five, mom. Dad died ten years ago," Leo reminded her.

"You should have grabbed Mrs. Ruggerio's Eileen. She was always crazy about you."

"No moustaches, Ma. It's where I draw the line."

She tilted her head back to work the bifocals. "Oh sure, the neighborhood girls weren't good enough for you."

He let her go on, wondering what it would be like when she died. He'd returned to Philly after her last stroke, determined to see her through to the end. Six years now and she never looked better.

"Your father was right." She handed him a beer from her little cooler. "You're a bungler, Leo. You could have joined the business, but no. You had to go to California. You had to marry every floozie who came down the pike. And to think we almost gave you up for adoption."

Leo slid in beside her on the sofa. "You're right, Mom. I should have been a salesman. I should have married Eileen Ruggerio, but …" he held up a finger, "… at least I didn't murder my mother, like Richie Pettis."

"Richie was a bastard, but he was no bungler." She gave him a poke. "Besides, who was it sent your father to an early grave, aanh?"

"He had emphysema, for Christ sake!"

"You know what I mean." The bifocals gave her a haughty look. Leo didn't know what she meant, but he let it pass. The smoke from her cigarette curled into a perfect circle. He never came without a carton, hoping against hope.

They ate microwaved chicken, raw on the inside. Leo could hear the clack of her dentures over the talk show radio. Afterwards, he did the dishes and put out the trash. Standing in her tiny yard, he raised his eyes to the South Philly skies. One star, way over Jersey.

"Star light, star bright, first star I see tonight," he tried to remember the rest. The light circled slowly and descended to the airport. When he returned, his mother was sound asleep in front of the TV. He leaned to kiss her forehead, slipped a twenty from her purse, and let himself out.

There was a postcard from Julie in the morning mail. "I love you, but I don't like you."

Benny was waiting for him at the diner. The Sheik, Julie called him, in reference to the do, jet black and raked back like it was painted on. Not a good look for Benny, nearing sixty and putting on the pounds.

"Where you been?" He hiked his eyebrows. "I'm on a schedule here."

"What schedule?" Leo checked the clock. "The tit bars don't open for hours."

"Yeah, OK, that's funny. Sit down, would you? I got a kink." Benny rubbed his neck.

"Maybe you should give the girls a break for a while. Everything in moderation, eh Sheik?"

"Yeah, that's funny."

"Not that it's pathetic or anything."

"I just thank God I lived to see the day. You only go around once, kid. Tell me a better way to spend the time?"

Leo smiled. "Well, it's good you found your niche."

"Tell me you got HD, Leo."

"What I got is ceiling fans. Top of the line and in the box."

Benny's eyebrows shot up higher. Everything was eyebrows with the Sheik.

"What the fuck am I gonna do with ceiling fans? What about the TVs?"

Leo tapped his pudgy little hand. "Next time, Benj. This time it's ceiling fans."

"Jesus, Leo. Tell me it ain't down to this."

"It's down to this, Benny." Leo flapped his hands around. "Hey, it beats scalping tickets, right?"

The Sheik sat there staring off. "I don't know what happened. What the fuck happened?"

"Prosperity, Benny." Leo shrugged. "It's a socio-economic thing."

"Jesus, I miss the old days. This ..." He shook his lacquered head.

"Benny, hey, these are top of the line fans here. You want in?"

He just kept shaking his head.

"Tell you what," Leo drummed his thumbs on the counter, "give me two grand for the whole load. That's one hundred units, plus remote."

"Units. God help us."

"I can deliver them or you can come pick them up. Your call."

The Sheik heaved a sigh and reached in his jacket. Leo waited but the hand just stayed there.

"Look at you," the old crook laughed. "Hey this reminds me of the scene in that movie where the guy reaches for his wallet and pulls out his gun."

"What movie? What are you talking about, Benny?"

"The movie where the hoods hijack a truckload of something, not ceiling fans. I forget."

"In or out, c'mon Benny."

"Coffins, that's what it was." Benny leaned in close. "Only some of them was occupied."

"Time's up." Leo stormed off, slowing slightly to give Benny an opening. When the bastard declined, he pushed through the door and crossed the lot to the black SUV. He felt out of focus, not all there, a flash to the 80's with his head full of Tester's. Not like Benny to queer a deal. Sheik could move broken glass and at the lowball price, he had to know Leo was desperate. What was it with the old guys that they got so goofy? The problem was, who else can you go to? The other problem was what to do with them now. The ceiling fans. They were in Ludlow's garage at the moment, but his wife was squawking and his neighbors were nosey. Not to mention Leo's sudden cash flow problem. He watched Benny through the window, willing him to change his mind. For a second he thought it just might work, but the fat fuck sat there feeding his face.

A Julie message on the machine.

"I think you should resolve your conflict with your mother. She won't be around much longer, you know."

Leo wondered who she could be staying with, and drew up a list of likely suspects. The thing that always bothered him, he could picture Julie with almost anyone. She came late to the cheating game, but it didn't take her long to get the hang of it. Catholic schoolgirl turning with a vengeance. He played the message a second time. The phone rang while he was looking at it.

"Leo?"

"Yeah Luds. I'm gonna move 'em, don't rip a stitch."

"That's what I called about. They're not here."

"What?"

"The ceiling fans. I came home tonight and they were gone,"

Leo pictured Ludlow's garage, the space they took up.

"I know you'll think I'm getting over, but someone stole them, Leo. I swear to fucking God."

"Someone walked off with a truckload of ceiling fans?"

"Fucking un-believable, right?"

Lying rat-fuck son of a bitch.

"You don't want to do this, Ludlow. Couple of days, they'll pop up, right?"

"On my father's fucking grave, Leo. Hey, I'm out just like you!"

Leo thought he heard someone else talking, but he couldn't be sure. He didn't want to think about what was happening here. Ludlow meant to beat him on the load.

"Couple of days. Ludsy. I'll give you a call."

The Phillies were in a rebuilding year. Except for one championship season, that shining moment decades past, the Phils had been rebuilding for over a century. Once again, pitching was the problem. Pitching was always the Phillies problem, except for the odd year when hitting was also the problem. Many like Leo saw the organization as genetically flawed, those fluke years in the 80's just a statistical anomaly. Throw the monkeys out on the diamond often enough, etc.

Only not THESE monkeys. Their record was more than a matter of bad judgment. Touted prospects shed their talent as they moved through the system. High school phenoms left their confidence and their fastballs in Spartansburg and Wilkes-Barre. Management, depending on the year and level of hostility, made one of two wrong moves. Either they let this year's wunderkind languish in the bush leagues, tying up time and money, or they rushed him into the rotation where he was promptly battered beyond recognition. Pick a year, same story.

Tonight's pitcher was a recent pickup from Houston. Front office couldn't resist these guys, the one season whiz with a flakey reputation, career castoffs cycling down. All too often it ended with the Phillies.

The first pitch was a strike, triggering visions of a strike-out. The season was young and hope springs eternal. The second pitch was strike two swinging and even the cynics allowed themselves to dream. Pitches three, four and five sailed up, up, and away and the rustle in the stands set the seasonal tone. After a confab with the catcher the castoff bore down, fucking beachball coming at ya. Leo could see the batter's eyes light up, then a white blur slicing down the right field line. The game quickly settled into a rout, brutal even by Phillie standards. The fans turned ugly early, taunting the castoff with death threats, burying him in boos when they yanked him in the second. Stunned by their rage, he stumbled off the field, disappearing into a dugout from which he would never again emerge.

A parade of relievers was promptly pounded.

By the seventh, the crowd sat in grim silence, reflecting on all things Philadelphian. Leo was aware of a disturbing parallel between the team's fortunes and his own. It was no coincidence that he spent the glory year in California, watching on TV. The implications were clear, and Leo had vowed never to go home again. If that was the price, he was willing to pay it. Julie, of course, had other ideas, his mom had her stroke and the rest was just history repeating itself. Of the teams who excelled at futility, none could touch those Fumblin' Phils. Losers of more games than any team in any sport.

Ever!

They were new and splashy, but they were still row houses. Two where three used to be, bay windows facing out on the drycleaners. Leo parked behind a row of pickups and listened for Lanny's blather.

"What the fuck is this? I got fucking monkeys working for me!"

Rear bedroom, upstairs. The front door was open, the downstairs rooms were bland and tasteless. Leo's own house had the original woodwork, circa 1917. He'd bought it for a song before he met Julie. The thing about modern, it lacked the detail. He waited for the windbag to take a breath, but Lanny was on an ass-chewing roll.

"Look at this! There's more fucking paint on the carpet than there is on the fucking wall!"

Leo watched from the doorway. A trio of Mexicans shrugged it all off.

"Nice ceiling fans," he called over.

"Heyyy! Leo my man!" Lanny broke it off and clapped him on the shoulder. "Whaddya think? Federal Terrace, my piece de resistance!"

"Where'd you get 'em Lanny?"

The big man took his arm and led him to the hallway. "Yo Leo, you workin' for L and I, or what?"

Leo hated this shit. "Tell me now while I'm still in a good mood."

Lanny looked more puzzled than worried. "Some guy came around. I didn't ask questions."

"Know something, boss?" Leo pointed with his chin. "Those amigos can't understand a thing you're saying."

Lanny looked in on the Mexicans and smiled. "Best fucking crew I ever had. They'd paint each other if I gave them the word."

"Tell me about this other guy. Do I know him?"

"I wasn't around. Maybe Pedro here can-"

"Cut the crap, Irish."

Lanny looked right through him. "I gotta tell you man, the tough stuff doesn't suit you."

He really hated this. Ludlow was making some kind of move, and betting Leo would roll over. Ceiling fans, for Christ sake!

"I got nothin' to do with this." Lanny stood his ground. "Hey, I'm just trying to make a living."

Leo left a footprint on the front door.

This was serious. Ludlow had always been flakey, but they'd been at this for thirty years. Leo called and got the machine. He drove over but no one answered the door. After that, he didn't know what to do. Ludlow tended bar on the Ave. The place was a dive, mostly ironworkers and off-duty cops. Not a place to start something, but what did Leo plan to start, anyway?

He went to McGrath's to think it through, but they had the game on and Shank was there and the night got away from him. Next morning he spotted Ludlow's truck in the diner lot. Leo signaled to turn but changed his mind, nearly clipping a roofing truck.

Julie again. Leo didn't even play it.

"Whaddya mean, whaddya do? You go after him!" Mario made a chopping motion. "You make him fucking pay!"

Leo stared at his hands. "I've known Ludlow all my life."

Mario stumbled to a chair, winded. "Everybody's known him all their lives. What's that got to do with it?"

"I don't want to hurt him."

"He's a piece of shit!"

"I don't have the time for this."

Mario gave him a poke. "That's what he's counting on, dude. You blow it off, you're out of business."

Leo looked at him. "What business? I'm peddling ceiling fans and eating at my mother's!"

Mario plopped his hands on the armrests. "I'm just saying, you take it from Luds, you take it from everyone. It's a business liability."

"He's a brick shithouse!"

"So, you pay somebody. Yo pal," he bent into Leo's line of vision, "this is pretty basic stuff."

He tried the number for the hundredth time. Ludlow answered on the fifteenth ring.

"Yeah what?"

"It's me, Leo."

Silence.

"We gotta talk, Luds."

"We got nothing to talk about. I told you, Leo, the fans were boosted."

Leo looked to Mario. Mario looked away.

"Mario says I should come after you." Leo ducked an empty beer can.

"Mario? That fucking lowlife?"

"But I say we can work this out. Like gentlemen, whaddya think, Luds?"

"Tell Mario to go fuck himself."

"I get my half and I forget all about it," Leo talked the talk.

"Come on, Lip, what are you gonna do? I say they were boosted, they were boosted. You can think whatever Mario wants you to."

"Don't do this, Ludsy."

"Gotta go."

A rainout forced a double header. Leo sat away from the crowd. He watched the game and thought about Luds and how he should have seen this coming. Ludlow was a crook. And Mario was right, once word got out, all accounts would go into arrears. Leo couldn't take a hit right now. He was living on credit cards as it was.

The Phils scored in the first. He thought of dropping a dime on Luds, then ruled it out. Then the cop are in and everyone's pissed, and he's out of business anyway. Should have gone to college with the rest of the goobers. Should have joined the fucking business. Had to be a hustler, no nine to five for Leo the Lip. Now Ludlow wanted to muscle in. Who muscled in on ceiling fans?

Pittsburgh scored three in the fifth and the Phils yanked the starter. Leo spotted Pete Newlin but pretended not to. Predictably, Pete failed to pick up on it.

"HEY LEO! HEY, RIGHT HERE!" He waved his arms and started over.

"Hey Newlin, I'm kinda busy right now."

"I just wanted to tell you, that Jackie Ludlow is an asshole."

"… Thanks."

"I told Dooley and them. I said you'd beat the balls off him."

"… Again, thanks."

"That fucker will rue the fucking day, yo!"

Pittsburgh scored three more in the eighth. Leo didn't stick around for game two.

Luds' truck was in the driveway. Leo circled the block a few times then parked in the church lot.

"OK, now what?" he asked himself.

Butch Isler had called offering his services. Not out of loyalty. Ludlow just pissed people off. Leo said he'd get back to him, but he knew he wouldn't. Even if he wanted to, he couldn't afford it. Big Butchie was top of the line.

By now, the news was all over Pennsport. The early line gave Leo the nod with an assist to Butchie. Every passing minute made it worse. If the other shoe didn't fall soon, he wouldn't be able to show his face.

And Ludlow was crazy. Once Leo made a move, it would be his turn and it wasn't hard to guess where the money would go on that. Which left what?

Dory answered the door, walked him to the yard like she didn't have a clue. Who was she kidding? Ludlow sat at the picnic table talking on the phone. He saw Leo in the doorway and rolled his eyes.

"Yeah, I know, that's why I'm calling," he growled into the phone. "You're damn right I'm pissed. Now how do you want to do it?"

Leo sat opposite. Ludlow yacked and yacked. Leo reached over and pressed the button.

"Hey Leo, what the fuck?"

"Sit down, Luds. Your neighbors are gawking."

"Fuck them, and fuck you too."

"What are you gonna do, hump around to every job site in the city?"

Ludlow smirked. "Face it, Leo, you've lost the touch. You let that old dago Bennie jerk you around for nickels on the dollar. I get forty a pop for 'em."

"OK, I see your point. Give me my grand and go peddle your wares."

"Or else what?"

Leo watched a small bird hop across the driveway. He thought of Julie lying in the sun on Goat Rock Beach. He got up from the table and shoved his hands in his pockets.

"Yo Luds. That's it?"

"Hey, we can go around and around, but basically, … yeah."

Leo left by the side gate. He could hear the big fuck laughing on the phone as he crossed the street. In his head, he saw himself go to the car and get his gun. One to the chest, one to the head was how you fixed these things. Only Leo didn't have a gun. The only time he ever shot a gun was on the boardwalk in Wildwood. Plus, if he killed Ludlow, he'd have to go to prison. No fucking way he was going to prison over ceiling fans.

Still, he thought about it.

On the way home he passed Zero and Lou on the Quarthouse corner. They fell all over themselves pretending not to see him.

In the morning Leo woke with a rock in his gut. He wondered about the way it was here, the deep end as the standard course of action. It wasn't normal, it couldn't be. This was as close to murder as Leo would get, but he knew it wasn't all that close. He could handle himself in a spot, but he didn't have a murder in him. He knew it, and Ludlow knew he knew it.

If there was a way out, Leo couldn't find it.

"So, I've been thinking …" Julie paused.

"OK."

"We could try it again, Leo. I know now that I need you."

"To what? Help you move?"

"OK, I deserve that. I know I was a shit about Mario, but he's so …"

"You gotta stop calling Julie. Please."

"You miss me, Leo. Marianne told me you hardly ever come out of the house."

Leo unplugged the phone. The next day he sold the SUV.

"Leo, hey! Jesus Christ! What's it been, what … ten years?"

"How are you Len? You look good."

"Hey! I heard you got married a while back. How's it working out?"

"It didn't." Leo shrugged. "I make a lousy husband."

"Tell me about it. I get a different set of kids every freaking weekend."

Leo took the chair across the desk. "I see your mug in the papers, real estate broker extraordinaire. You've done well, Len."

He gave his paunch a pat. "Well, I can't complain. But you didn't come all the way down here to sing my praises. What is it I can do for you, Leo?"

"I want to sell."

Len looked offended. "Your place? It's a jewel box, man. I can't let you do it!"

"Got to. I owe some money. Plus, I think my ex has her eye on a slice."

"Well, she'll get that, friend. Community property."

"Maybe not. It's still in my name."

Lenny's gaze dropped to his shoes. "Jeez, I don't know, Leo. It sounds unethical."

Leo pulled a wad from his pocket and slapped it on the desk. "One thousand up front. Plus, five percent."

Len didn't even look at the money. "Maybe we can finagle something."

"It's gotta be fast. All offers considered, I'll take the hit. And I'd like it to be someone, you know … responsible."

"I have that someone in mind as we speak."

"And no sign. It's gotta be discrete."

"I think I can handle this for you without much problem, Leo."

"Like I said. Extraordinaire."

Leo walked away with 150 thou. Not bad for the old neighborhood, bless the Irish and their woodwork. He left a message on Gail's machine and stashed 50 grand in his mother's account. He'd send an address when he turned up. Palm Beach, maybe. Hustle the widows. Or Tempe. He heard it was nice in Tempe.

DARK AND STORMY NIGHT

It was summer when he finally showed up. Larry worked the night shift then and Nicole was still a baby. Gina was at the kitchen window watching raindrops plink the puddles when she heard a rumble outside the front door. She knew right away it was him, though she could never say how. There were always cars idling in the street at night, boyfriends of neighborhood girls giving it one last shot, suburban kids copping a bag. They cursed too much and laughed too loud, and their flashers kept her up at night.

This was different; she could tell by the sound. This one moved down the street at a crawl, and as it paused outside her door, she saw a match flare inside. Her first impulse was to grab Nicole and run, but something held her to the spot. She watched the headlights sweep across the yard as he turned into the driveway. Instead of stopping at the garage, he pulled the car behind the house, killed the lights and the motor, and sat listening to the radio. Basie, she thought, or one of those swing bands he favored. A sound she hadn't heard in years.

When he got out, Gina's heart was pounding so loud she could hear it. He circled to the front of the car and opened the hood. She could see rain roll off his back as he fiddled inside. Whatever was wrong, he fixed it quickly, then stood staring up at the back of the house. Still tall and rangy in a leather jacket, jeans and work boots.

Six years since she'd heard a word.

She opened the door before he could knock.

"Hey Gina. It's me, Pete. How's my girl?"

"I'm not your girl."

He had an answer for this. She could see it in his face. But the words wouldn't come and instead, he just stood there blinking into the rain.

"I'm in a fix, kid."

"You go to hell."

"I got you something." He pulled a small box from his jacket and handed it to her. Good & Plenty's, half empty.

"Jeepers, thanks Dad," she turned and tossed it in the trash.

"It's short notice, baby. Hell hounds are on my trail."

"Where's Corrine?"

"Back in Florida with her mom." He shrugged. "I guess she couldn't hack it anymore."

The news didn't hit like it should have. Corrine was the reason he'd left them flat, and Gina always prayed she'd get fat, or die. From the time she was a girl until it didn't matter anymore.

"You can't stay here."

"Is that what you think? Gina, honey, you got nothing to worry about. I just want to see my grandchild. Then I'll be on my way."

She let him stand there until he was soaked, doorknob warming in her hand, steam rising from the hood of the car. This was nothing like she thought it would be.

"Look Gina, I know you don't want anything to do with me. I used to think someday I'd make it all up to you. I don't know. When you're young, you believe anything's possible. You know what I'm saying?"

"I learned a long time ago to leave it alone."

He glanced away, following the taillights of a passing car.

"OK. I guess I always had an unrealistic view of life. I can understand why you hate me."

"Hate you? I don't even know you."

Just the way she'd always rehearsed it, studying her reflection in the mirror for the perfect look. Proud and contemptuous, the glib tone to cut to the quick.

"Yeah well, it's probably just as well."

Gina just looked at him.

"How is she? The baby?"

"She's asleep. Thunder had her up half the night."

"I'd be grateful if you'd let me in for a minute."

"I told you to go to hell." She pushed the door shut and that was that.

Except he wouldn't leave, wouldn't even get back in the car. For over an hour, he sat on the stoop letting the rain pour down on him. She watched from upstairs, biting hard on her lip to keep it together. Seeing him stirred up memories she'd kept buried for years. Not forgotten, but sealed off in a part of her heart she'd put off limits. The night he showed up in a limo full of presents. God only knows where they came from; a portable TV for her and a tricycle for Bette, a diamond pendant and earrings for their mom. They'd driven to the shore that very night, passing through those sleepy Jersey towns like desperados, hitting the boardwalk just as the sun was rising. The police picked him up the next day at their beachfront hotel. Her mom pawned the jewels for the cab ride home.

So long since she'd let herself drag it all up, but time had failed to dim the image. Her recollections of him were as worn and dog-eared as an old paperback.

"It's not the feds I'm worried about. They're like elephants. You can hear them coming a mile away."

"I don't want to hear this, OK?" She was still angry with herself for letting him in.

"Sorry baby," he gave her that crow's feet grin. "Tell me about your husband. Does he know about me?"

"He knows you ran off. The rest doesn't really bear mentioning."

He laughed. "You always did have that sledgehammer touch."

"Larry's a good man who loves his wife and kid. End of story."

"What about you? Do you love him?"

Leave it to Pete to ask the one question she couldn't answer. What she had with Larry was good, but she'd seen love burn as hot as fire.

"Larry and me are doing fine."

"I should shove off before he comes home."

"He doesn't get off for a few hours yet," she poured him more coffee. "I thought you wanted to see your granddaughter."

"More than anything in this world."

"How'd you find out about her?"

He took a single bent Camel from his shirt pocket and rolled it straight on the table.

"I looked up your sister when I was on the coast. I told her I was coming here."

"Bette didn't say anything to me."

"I made her promise not to. I figured the less time you had to think about it, the less likely you were to shoot me."

"I'm partial to knives actually."

Again, the grin. "Bette said you had a hard time of it. With the baby I mean."

"Yeah well, they come into the world kicking and screaming. If they knew what was out here, they'd think twice about it."

"You can't really mean that."

"You can't smoke in here."

She led him down the hall to the baby's room. Nicole lay sleeping on her stomach with her hands balled in tiny fists. He reached down to touch her head.

"So much hair for such a new baby."

"She gets that from Larry's side. That, and her temperament."

"What does she get from you?"

"Fear of thunder. I don't know, flatulence?"

"Your mom used to swear she never once broke wind. She claimed she didn't even have an asshole until she married me."

Gina had to laugh, and laughing made her think of what this must look like. Three generations of Perkins in the same room. It had never occurred to her that this could happen, and now that it had, she could feel the tug of kinship, sweet and unbearably sad. He was running out of time, or he wouldn't be here.

"I'd wake her but there'd be hell to pay."

"That's fine. I just want to look."

He stroked the side of the baby's face, running his finger from cheek to jaw line. Gina couldn't help herself. She moved up close and brought her hands to his shoulders. Pete was all skin and bone. Lowering her head to his back, she breathed him in, leather and smoke, the flesh of her flesh. It was all too much for her. She was already crying when he turned and took her in his arms. Folded her away just like a real dad.

"Baby, don't," he whispered in her ear.

"I can't help thinking it could have been like this," she sobbed into his jacket. "I just want to hear you say it could have been like this. Please."

"Gina, honey, you're killing me."

"Say it, dammit!" she hissed, and broke away, pounding his chest like a B movie spitfire. Pete twisted away from her, stumbled off a few steps, then crumpled to a heap on the floor. He lay gasping on his side, and she could see the blood though his open jacket.

"Oh my god! You're hurt!"

He rolled to his knees and hugged himself against the pain. His face was pale and sweaty, and she was certain he'd die right there on the spot. Instead, he pulled himself up slowly by the baby's crib and turned to her with his right hand raised.

"It's not as bad as it looks," he murmured, his grin fading to a grimace. "But no more hitting, OK?"

She did what she could, cleaned the wound then closed it up with a box of butterfly band-aids she found in the bathroom.

He'd wanted her to stitch him, but her hands were too shaky and her stomach wasn't up to it. Pete sat at the table talking non-stop while she dressed him with Pampers and strips of duct tape.

"I've known some bad boys, but these guys are murder. I thought he was just a card cheat."

"What guys?"

"Skip tracers. They contract out to bail bondsmen for a percentage. Do yourself a favor baby, don't ever jump bail."

"Here, hold this." She handed him the scissors and worked the tape over his shoulder. "You should be in a hospital."

"I must be losing my feel for people. Back in the day I would have smelled him out in a crowd. Thing is, he had intellect. The man read Gaddis, for Christ sake!"

"You knew him?"

"We ran a high stakes game in Reno. He beat the bushes and I fleeced the bunnies. He knew he had me anytime, so he rode it out."

"So he's a crook too?"

"He's a bounty hunter. Mostly they're ex-cops or mercenaries. A hell of a thing to do for a living."

"Do they work with the police?"

"Not if they can help it. They might serve notice, but they don't carry badges and they don't need warrants."

"How much you owe?"

"Enough to make it worth their while. But it's not like you can just pay them back," he pulled the bloody shirt back on and leaned forward in his chair. "There's no negotiating, believe me. And they're not like cops. They love what they do."

"Maybe you should turn yourself in."

"I've been tempted, if only to cut them out of the deal."

She stuffed the scraps of tape and diaper in a plastic bag and crossed the kitchen to the trash bin.

"Don't." He reached out his hand. "I'll take that with me when I leave."

"You're hurt pretty bad, Pete. You need a doctor."

"Got one waiting for me down in Knoxville. His eyes aren't what they used to be, but he still takes my health insurance."

She knelt by his side, took his hand and held it to her face. Might be she'd never see him again, and she wanted to take in as much as she could. She touched his fingers to her own cheek, then turned his hand over. The knuckles of his thumbs were swollen with arthritis, but his nails were clean and freshly manicured.

"Stay the night. I'll tell Larry you're an old cousin or something. I don't think you'll make it to Knoxville."

"I appreciate it, honey. Thing is, these guys have eyes and ears where you'd never expect. I'm OK as long as I keep moving."

"You don't think they'll come here, do you?"

"Nobody knows I have family. I go by different names. Before I left Reno, I made a few calls to an old pal in Tahoe. With any luck, they'll be dropping in to see him."

"Gee thanks, old pal."

"I meant that figuratively," he gave her a wink.

She made him breakfast, scrambled eggs and bacon done crisp the way she knew he liked it. Her mother had never been much of a cook, and had left the kitchen work to her daughters. Gina remembered making breakfast for Pete and his cronies. She'd get up early and arrange everything on the counter, then watch cartoons until she heard them pull up outside. She'd make cheese omelets or French toast, with orange juice and plenty of strong coffee. The men shoveled in all she could make, plying her with praise and proposals of marriage. They may have been crooks, but they treated her like a queen, and there were always a few bucks on the table when they were through. Sometimes they'd sing to her, doo wop harmonies from when they were boys, or one of a half dozen drinking songs, a morning serenade that would carry her through the whole day. Then they'd leave in a swirl of laughter and cigarette smoke, pulling away with horns honking, long after the other dads had gone to work. When she thought of Pete, she thought of mornings. After he left, just looking at the skillet could bring her to tears.

"Was Bette glad to see you?"

"Hard to say. I know she was surprised."

"What's her place like? I've never been there."

"Nice place. Her hubby's rolling in it. Funny thing is, I did some work for his father back in the seventies. He had a few shipments go bad on the docks and he needed them to disappear."

"But she met Jack at Cal."

"What can I tell you? It's a small world, kid."

She thought back to the globe he gave her one Christmas, black oceans and green continents with a pin sticking right out of New Jersey.

"So what, you've been living out west?" she asked him.

"Nah, the coast doesn't suit me. Too much sun makes a man simple."

"This thing in Reno. When did it happen?"

"We left there over a week ago. He waited until Chicago to make the bust. Had me handcuffed to a motel television, so I picked the lock. About this time yesterday. That's another thing. I gotta get rid of that car."

"You took his car?"

"It's a rental. I'll drop it off in Knoxville after I see the doc."

"What did you do to him? The bounty hunter."

"He'll be alright. Too bad, though. We could have cleaned up in Branford. The kid had some class."

While she did the dishes he studied a map, tracing his route with a yellow highlighter. Outside, the rain had stopped and the sky was turning gray. The car in the yard looked cold and forlorn, and it pained her to think it was down to this for him; a stolen car, a vague destination. She saw his reflection in the window as he came up behind her, and she knew she would always look for him there.

"You're right, Gina. It could have been like this." He kissed the top of her head. "I got my share of regrets, that's for sure."

She turned and looked him in the face. "Will I ever see you again?"

"Honey, there's no doubt about it."

Lightning flashed outside the window and a loud crack of thunder shook the dishes in the drain board. She slipped past Pete to check on the baby. Nicole was looking straight up at the ceiling, gurgling on a mouthful of fingers. More thunder rolled right over top of them, breaking off somewhere to the west. Still, Nicole did not cry. Gina couldn't know it, but years would pass before she'd see her baby cry again. And then, only when they buried her Grampa Pete.

She picked up Nicole and wrapped her in a blanket. The baby's smile seemed to light up the room. Lightning flashed as they made their way up the hallway. When they got to the kitchen, he was just driving off.

ACCOMPLICE

Frankie takes the 41 to the end of the line, steps off into a twilight of chirping crickets and fresh cut grass. He walks past Tudor mansions and sprawling haciendas feeling more than a little conspicuous. In the fading light, he sees kids on trail bikes circling a cul de sac. A dog barks. A pool filter hums. Dishes clatter in a kitchen sink.

The house at 105 Pennridge Court has a pillared front porch. Whistling a one-note tune, Frankie passes by without a glance. He continues on to a grove of trees at the end of the block, picks one with an unobstructed view and shimmies up to a forty-foot perch. A hedge runs along the rear of the house. Lights are on in an upstairs room, and a TV flickers through a downstairs window.

Cassie's house reminds Frankie of his grandparents' place in Pennsylvania. He remembers chasing his cousin through piles of raked leaves while his mom and his grandmother battled inside. His mother grew up in a neighborhood like this, a fact that never ceases to amaze him. Once, while searching for her dope stash, he stumbled on a shoebox filled with old photographs, Christmas snapshots of Sandy and siblings. He keeps the best one in his wallet, her big eyes and uncertain smile. Already life was proving unmanageable.

Frankie wonders about his mother's latest transformation – Madame Sandra, Sayer of Sooth. Cassie was her first client, and Frankie's favorite, but there are others, long-limbed girls with designer checkbooks. Their cars beam brightly between the gutted wrecks of Beck Street. They huddle with Madame Sandra, ignoring Frankie completely. Fact is, his mother has changed in ways miraculous. Bills get paid. Meals are somewhat regular. Actual routines are taking shape. Lately, when he looks in her eyes, he sees more than his own reflection. Frankie's hopeful, but at thirteen he knows he's young enough to be fooled.

When it's dark, he climbs down from his perch and makes his way to the edge of the woods. The streets are empty. He walks with his head down, feeling invisible. At 105 he turns up the drive, then veers across the back yard to the hedge. He squats in the bushes, recalling his instructions.

"Just take a look around. See what goes on over there." Sandy slipped a dollar bill in his pocket. "Keep out of sight and don't steal anything."

"And if I get caught?"

"Don't get caught, honeybunch. We're talking meal ticket here."

She confides in him now. At first the palms were a problem for her. They all looked alike and revealed nothing. But there are easier ways to gauge the fates. An unsolicited trash pickup revealed a preference for imported vodka and ribbed condoms. An intercepted mail delivery spelled out details of a messy divorce and messier settlement. If the future is unforeseeable, the past is as plain as this month's phone bill. In just a few weeks Madame Sandra has learned more about life at 105 Pennridge Court than Cassie knows herself.

Frankie leans his head against the house, feels the TV volume vibrate through the wall. A light clicks on in the window above him. A shadow passes to the snap of elastic. Frankie throws caution to the wind and sneaks a peek. Cassie stands in her underwear making faces in the bathroom mirror. Faces of cold calculation and smoldering desire, faces she will never use. Then a sudden crunch of gravel and headlights sweep over the yard. Frankie ducks and rolls under the hedge, flattening a day-old mound of dog shit. The stench is sudden and stupendous, and he buries his face in the dirt to escape it. The car swings around the circular drive, stopping less than ten feet away. Two people get out, a man and a woman.

"Whoooeee!" the man fans the air. "Rusty must have just pinched one off."

"Oh, that goddamn dog is ruining my pachysandra," Cassie's mom gripes. They start for the house but the man pauses, so close Frankie could untie his shoes.

"Jesus," he gasps. "Have you checked him for worms lately?"

"It's shit, Roy. Let's not dwell on it."

"Sorry, love. Wouldn't dream of it." He hastens to join her.

As the door swings shut, Frankie scrambles to his knees spewing mac and cheese over his shoes. His breath catches in a gag and he whirls in circles pulling at his sweatshirt. Weak and wheezy, icy with sweat, he crawls off trailing pachysandra and coagulating gobs of goo. Inside, voices rise and fall, carrying through the siding like voices in a dream, Cassie and her mother going at it. At first Frankie can't make out what they're saying, but when they move to the corner room, their words become clear.

"Rodrigo? Who the hell is Rodrigo?" her mother is shouting.

"Come on, Mom! I told you. I met him at Tiffany's party. You said I should try and meet new people."

"American people! Jesus, do I have to spell everything out for you?" The mother's heels hammer the hardwood. "People named Rodrigo make minimum wage!"

"So that's it! You're a bigot! What about things like equality?"

"Equality is for your hot pants girlfriends, baby, not for you."

Their voices fade as they climb the stairs, but rise again from the second floor.

"You're ruining my life! I want to go live with Daddy."

"That's a laugh. Your father will have your Rodrigo deported."

They rant from room to room, then a door slams and silence stretches. Frankie shivers in the darkness. He wills himself to move, but nothing comes of it. The porch door squeaks and Roy steps out, stands at the rail looking up at the night sky. Frankie follows his gaze to a sliver moon, but when he looks back Roy's gone. Frankie strains to hear but no sound comes. His ears pound and his arms and legs stiffen. Roy must have spotted him. He's hiding out there waiting. He's sneaking up with a dagger in his teeth.

Frankie rips through the bushes, hurtles the hedge and clears the driveway in world-class time. Running blind, he somehow misses the lawn chairs and glass topped table, the marble birdbath and brick barbecue. Wind whistles in his ears and his feet barely touch the ground. He hits the clothesline chest high like a sprinter hits the tape. A fraction of his life flashes, then a million stars explode in his head.

The day's first 41 pulls up to Pennridge Court at daybreak. Frankie climbs aboard clutching a single dollar bill.

"Got no change, little brother," the driver looks him over.

"Keep it." Frankie struggles to stuff the bill in the fare box.

"No man, you keep it," the driver grins. "Since you lost the last round, I'm gonna let you ride for free. Just sit in back and open a window. The early birds are gonna love you."

Frankie pulls himself along by the handrail. The motion makes him dizzy and the lights hurt his eyes. He sticks his head out the window, but it doesn't help. Slouching low, he lifts his shirt and glances down at the braided welt embossed in clothespins.

"OH MY GOD, WHAT HAVE THEY DONE TO YOU?" Madame Sandra screeches like a worn set of brakes. Frankie staggers through the kitchen and collapses on the living room sofa.

"OH MY GOD, NOT ON MY SOFA!" Her cries rip across his brain. Contusions and abrasions vie for his attention. His clothes are crusted in filth and his head looks curiously lopsided. He feels worse than he looks.

"What have they done to you? How did this happen?" Madame Sandra flies around the room raining cigarette ashes over the rug. He tries to track her movements but his eyes refuse to rotate.

"It's OK, Mom," he croaks. "No one saw me."

"No one saw you? I suppose you did this to yourself?"

"It's OK," he tells her again. "It's OK." He can say it without moving his lips.

"Tell me what happened. Did you find out anything?" Madame Sandra pulls up a chair and sits facing him. "Cassie called last night. She was upset, but she wouldn't say why. She'll be over this afternoon and I need something to tell her."

"Rodrigo," he whispers.

"What? … Rodrigo?" She leans over and shakes his leg. "Hey, talk to me. Who is Rodrigo?"

"Cassie … boyfriend … big fight with mom." Frankie's lips stick together with every "b".

"This Rodrigo, where did she meet him? Do you know? … FRANKIE!" She pounds his leg with her fist.

"Party … Tiffany …" He lets his head fall back. Something pops in his neck as his eyeballs settle painfully in their sockets.

"A beaner boyfriend? Oh baby, that's fantastic!" She claps her hands, and a thousand bazookas explode in his head. Madame Sandra rushes off, and he hears her crooning on the telephone. Frankie stares up at the ceiling. The neon palm buzzes in the window.

DOG DAYS

Like most dictators, my father cloaked his intentions in the guise of democracy. As his subjects, we were consulted only after decisions had been made. We could see, even then, that the process was a sham, but the thread of his logic made dissent impossible. Whatever he proposed would be good for us in the long run, he reasoned, providing us with yet another thing he never had as a boy. Whether the pitch was for a new house or a new baby sister, our objections were duly noted and roundly ignored. Despite her seeming surprise at his pronouncements, my mother was the main pinsetter in negotiations, her protests serving only to define obligations, all of them ours. It wasn't the best system. It wasn't even a good system.

He preferred a captive audience for these deliberations and to this day, the phrase "a Sunday drive" is family lexicon for "breaking the news." Heads bowed and shoulders slumped, we would take up our positions in the back seat of the family car, (assigned, left to right in descending order). My father spoke to each of us through the rear view mirror. More often than not, we returned home fundamentally changed.

The very first Sunday drive covered the shortest distance, inches possibly, but forever set the tone. We were six, seven, and eight, and living in Long Island. Ike was president, Pious 12 was Pope, and the Dodgers were still in Brooklyn. Had we known the vagaries of fate, we would have marveled at our luck. Too late for the war, too early for the Red Scare, and just in time for television. The baby boom provided us with kids our own age, and the gods gave us Disney. What could go wrong?

That year's car was a two tone green Mercury with green interior, and an automatic gear shift to accommodate my mother. As the tallest, I was rear window left, behind my father. I would stare at his neck bulging over starched white collar. Study his hairline, and the crosshatched creases that deepened or faded when he moved his head. If the sun was right, I could track the capillaries in his ears, and when he rolled down the window to let fly with a loogie, I could see it wobble, then catch the wind.

"Larry! Must you?"

"Sorry dear."

I remember all of it.

Sunday Drive #1:

"All set?" he chirps, ignoring our descending looks of trepidation. We've been forced to face his directives en masse, and the alliance makes us uneasy. My sister is the first to flinch.

"I have to pee," she claims.

"This won't take long. You can hold it," he slips the car into gear.

"Noooo, I gotta gooooo."

He hits the brakes and we tumble backward. The car sputters, then stalls.

"Larry!"

"Sorry, Dear." He grinds the ignition to no avail. The silence marked by the whistle of his breathing, the ping of the dashboard clock, my mother tapping a cigarette against her thumbnail.

"It's flooded," he says, but we know he's guessing. He drums his wedding ring against the steering wheel and hums a line from Fernando's Hideaway. After a full minute, he tries again. Nothing.

"OK, listen up," he wades right in. "How would you guys feel about moving?"

"Nooooo," my sister wails. "Nooo, don't make us!"

"Not right away," he backpedals. "I'm thinking maybe next year."

"No, no, no."

"Maybe in the fall."

My brother turns away, staring out rear window right as if we're moving. My father can fit just two of us in the mirror without turning it, something he will do when the time comes.

"Why don't you say something?" My sister scowls at me.

"What good will it do?"

He turns the mirror.

"What do you think Bobby?"

My brother pushes the lock button down, pulls it up, pushes it down.

"Well, this is certainly going well," my mother sighs.

"They're just worried about leaving," he tells her. "Wait till they hear where we're going."

"Where are we going?" My sister stiffens.

"Pennnnnn – sylvania!" he announces like a train conductor.

"Nooooo, we don't want to."

"You'll love it. It's the country."

Why he thinks we will love it is a mystery. We know nothing of the country, though the case could be made that we know nothing of the city either. We know where our friends live, and how to go to the supermarket. We've heard of Pennsylvania, but couldn't find it on a map. We couldn't find any place on a map. We are only six, seven, and eight, but we are set in our ways.

"It's not definite," my mother assures us. What she means is, *It's definite*.

My sister sobs. "If we move, I'll kill myself."

"Come on now, Kitten." Dad's taken to calling her kitten after some father on TV.

"I'll take poison. We all will."

I picture the can of Drano under the sink, the blue skull and crossbones. I see us barricaded in the bathroom, my sister doling out portions.

"I don't get it." My father shakes his head. "When I was a kid, I would've given my eyeteeth to live in the country."

His willingness to part with eyeteeth is a matter of record, one of a dozen family slogans that bristle with imagery. My mother's "crack your head open" recalling eggshell skull shards, yokey brains spilling out. While other dads might part with an arm or a leg, eyeteeth were the coin of my father's realm.

"You think I would ask you to do something you wouldn't like?"

The loaded question; liking what he made us do rarely figured into things, as far as we could see. How else to explain the crew cuts and matching outfits, the argyle socks? That he would suggest otherwise signals a change in the ground rules. Bending the facts to fit your position was a dangerous precedent. That it would become the bedrock of my father's parenting strategy was fairly predictable.

"We'll jump off the roof!" my sister threatens.

Again, the bathroom, curtains wafting through an open window, heads cracked open down below.

"That's enough, young lady." He levels a finger at her reflection. "You'll do what I say, and you'll damn well like it!"

This last part is unlikely. We will do what he says because we are small and without weapons.

"What about school? What about our friends?" she flails away.

"You'll make new friends in a new school."

The grossest assumption yet; making friends is a perilous business. We'd seen enough new classmates thrown into the mix to know the position was tenuous. A single miscalculation and you were stuck with the fat kid.

"Oh pleeeease, oh pleeeease, oh pleeease don't make us!"

Dad gives the Mercury one last crank. The ignition grinds a wobbly vibrato, then trails off in a death rattle. My mother stares straight ahead, planning her escape.

"Whaddya say Bobby-boy. Help me out here," he pivots the mirror.

My brother works the button, his lips moving in silent incantation.

In Pennsylvania, our Sunday drives are different. He favors back roads through rolling farmland, River Drive to points unknown. The dreaded country - home to deer, possibly antelope, and myriad, fur-bearing body parts splattered about. My father drives with his arm across the seat, fingers tapping rhythm where my mother's head would be. My sister is at rear window right owing to my brother's recent growth spurt. We have a Buick now, an aberration in pink and green. How it came to be ours is never explained.

"Awful quiet back there."

Dead quiet, in fact. It's not like anything good ever comes of this. Last time out, he got lost, and we ended up getting braces. Once brought to our attention, our silence captures every sound: the drone of tires, the rustle of clothes. I feel my brother shudder beside me, and then he is humming, softly at first, then loud enough to throw my father's fingers off the beat. A one-note version of the Pepsodent jingle, only slower and less enthusiastic. It's not much, but it's something.

"You guys ever wonder what it would be like to have a dog?" asks Dad, way too casually. What it would be like to have a dog is of little interest to us. The few dogs we've known have been old or incorrigible. My aunt had a poodle that would drink martinis, but he died long before we could appreciate it. We sense that we are not dog people, just as we sense that we are not rich. Adjustments have been made.

"Tom?"

"What for?" I can only think to ask.

"What for? That's what you wonder?"

" ... Yeah."

"Let me tell you something, son. When I was your age I would've given my eyeteeth for a dog."

When I picture him at my age, he's just a smaller version of himself, the kid in the suit with the five o'clock shadow.

"What if we don't want one?"

"Jesus, am I missing something here? What kind of kids don't want a dog?"

The kind who hedge their bets. Since the decision has been made for us, we can only go on record. In fact, it's not a dog we don't want. It's the dog he will get us, defective in some way vital, impossible to assimilate. When left to his own devices, my father's judgment is notorious, the Buick being an obvious example.

"Dogs aren't easy, Dad," I say, as if anything he wants for us will ever be easy.

"What are you talking about? Dogs are practically self-sufficient."

"What about vet bills?"

"And ticks," my sister chimes in.

"And law suits," brother Bob, ever-practical.

"What about Old Yeller?" Dad counters. "Tell me you didn't love that son of a gun."

"Yeah, but they had to shoot him."

"And we don't even have a gun."

" ... Do we?"

Silence again as he considers a different approach, the three of us running down the list of TV dogs: too big, too pushy, too devoted. My father drifting into some misguided reverie, his giggly brood tumbling past the picture window with Old Yeller II, rushing to tell him of the latest trick, the newest adventure, cheeks rosy and eyes bright with gratitude.

"Patty Boyer's dog chases cars."

"Donald Hewitt's dog rolls in dead things."

"Mom wouldn't like it."

A low blow, perhaps, but positions must be clear on this. In the not-so-distant future when he's fixing the blame, it will be all we have. We don't want a dog. That practically said, we are weary of our Sunday drive, and anxious to return home to our last dog-less days. Instead, my father takes the turnoff to Vista Point, circles the empty parking lot, and kills the motor.

"I gotta tell you guys," he turns to face us. "This doesn't seem normal to me."

As if living in a wasteland of half-finished houses is normal. As if wrestling your dad into bed every night is normal. A pink car with green interior, this is normal?

"Are you mad at us?" My sister does her kitten voice.

"No, not mad so much as … disappointed."

We try our best to look contrite.

"I was sure you'd be tickled pink."

"Maybe when we're older," brother Bob consoles him.

"I just want you to be happy, you know?"

"We are," we practically whimper.

The dog is a white boxer, full grown with a nubby tail and great yellow teeth. He is there when we get home from school, tied to a stake in the backyard. His relentless yelp echoed all the way to the bus stop, draining the blood from my sister's face. We trudge up the driveway like condemned prisoners. The dog charges the second he sees us, nearly garroting himself with my mother's clothesline.

"Isn't he something?" my father calls from the safety of the porch.

He is that. 70 pounds if he's an ounce, and standing in at throat level, though it's difficult to tell with him writhing around like that. The yelp reduces to a gurgle as he grapples with the clothesline, our very own Hound of the Baskervilles, Old Yeller with rabies.

"What should we do?" My sister looks to me. I know that she will run if I say the word.

"Don't be afraid. Dogs can smell fear."

"But I am afraid."

"Then don't stand here." I nudge her towards my brother.

"What's the matter with you guys?" My father steps away from the porch. "Come over and say hello."

We stay where we are, my sister mewling softly, my brother gnawing his lower lip. We are thinking the same thing. In years to come, when we recall Dad being torn to pieces, it will begin this way. Watching him close the distance, the long ash of his cigarette, the tinkle of ice in his glass. For some reason he is in his socks and I hear that bone snapping in his ankle, as much my father's sound as change in a pocket or wingtips over a hardwood floor. The dog backs away, clawing at the clothesline, yanking his head from side to side. When he runs out of rope, my father moves in, but the dog scrambles quickly to the right, circling the stake in a snarling frenzy. The pull of the collar yanks his ears forward, loose skin bunching in folds above his nose. He moves to the right when my father moves left, then left as my father moves right. He is better at this than my father is.

"One of you give me a hand," he calls over to us.

Fat chance, mister. We are versed well enough in the fine print of the fourth commandment to know the loopholes. Honor thy father, except when it will get you killed.

"Just grab the rope," my brother tells him.

To our surprise, he does just that. He crouches to reel the dog in, then, failing that, pulls himself closer, hand over hand. The struggle grows fierce as the angles diminish, and then suddenly the dog is free. A white streak across the back yard, over tractor rutted mud flats, past the long line of houses in progress, fading in the distance like the pale dot of a TV screen.

My father stands with his back to us, clutching the last few feet of clothesline. The empty collar dangles limply at the end. I can read what he's thinking in the tilt of his head, and I worry suddenly that he will just give up. This is, after all, the unspoken fear. Living with one parent is like living with one eye. The other one goes and it's lights out.

STRAIGHT LIFE

The week before the break, he got Lucille to white out the names and dates on her birth certificate. Told her to make a copy and type in a new name, any name, as long as it was easy to remember. She picked Buck Clayton, and that's who he is. You'd think having the same name as a famous jazzman would get you some attention in life, but you would be mistaken. Only twice has someone made the connection, and one of them had the wrong horn. Such is jazz fame.

Lucille left the birth certificate in the glove compartment along with a hundred dollars, a change of clothes, and a short note.

Dear Buck

Lotsa luck

He still carried the note in his wallet though he hadn't seen Lucille in 30 years.

He'd just turned twenty-four when he walked away. Half a mile through scrub pines to the local MacDonalds and a brown VW with the keys inside. Lucille was as good as her word. He

142

changed clothes in the parking lot, ordered a Big Mac with fries, and drove off to his new life in his own goddamn car.

In Denver, he hooked up with a girl in a bar. Couldn't remember her name, but never forgot the way she moaned when he took her from behind. Had her knock on the door a few minutes after he'd gone in to see the notary, and while the man was distracted, he slipped the seal from the desk. Spent a month in Reno waiting for the driver's license, then on to California for the Jerry Brown years.

Got the checks, got the food stamps, and at the end of six months, enrolled in nursing school for the standard six bits. Didn't use, didn't steal, and steered clear of the low life. Every move he made, he thought of Dexter. Breaking out was the easy part, Dex would say. It's staying out that most can't manage. Buck chose nursing for the ratio of women to men. In a year's time, he was managing nicely.

He met a girl named Peyton in a health food store, and within the year, made her Peyton Clayton. Funny thing, all those nurses and he marries a lawyer. They bought a house in a small town on the Carquinez Straits across the street from a massive weeping willow. The man who owned the tree said he stuck a branch in the ground on his wedding day. Three grown girls and a grandson later, that old tree was a hundred feet high. The man's name was Jack Walters. On the day Buck's son was born, he stuck three of Jack's branches in his front yard. It'd been over a year since he'd seen his son, but he could see those willows a mile away.

They were regulars at Juanita's Saloon, where they would sit on the back porch and watch the tankers slip past. Buck kept a bucket of flat stones out by the railroad tracks, and would skip them over the water and off the hulls, a distant bonk followed by curses from the crew. After his punchout with a biker from Hayward, Juanita named a drink after him. The Bloody Buck - a Bloody Mary double with Old Bay and clam juice served in a mason jar with a single spicy string bean. The Bloody Buck was an instant sensation, and over the years, it made her a bundle. Buck declined the brass barstool and commemorative plaque, but as long as Juanita owned the place, the Claytons drank for free. Saturday nights, they'd close the bar and join her across the street for an absinthe or two. Just the thing for the walk home. Buck's hand in Peyton's back pocket. Main Street in the moonlight, and not a car in sight.

Peyton quit the downtown firm and opened a practice at a nearby community center. It meant living on less, but the hours were better, and she was home for their son. Her work involved her in local issues, and their house became a gathering place for artists and activists. Jake was a California kid. Buck watched him grow, and marveled at how easy it was for him: parents who loved him, money coming in, every day as perfect as the day before. He worried that Jake wouldn't be ready for the harder knocks. He was a good kid and smart as a whip, but he didn't know what his old man knew.

Buck worked the ETC unit at Martinez General. It was an easy job with good benefits, but the days were long, and he missed being home. He helped a neighbor put an addition on his house to see how it was done, then put one on his own just to see if he could do it. He learned enough in the process to sideline as a home inspector. Loved crawling around in people's houses and giving it to them straight. Bought a truck and some overalls, and when the developers came, Buck was sitting pretty.

In the years Jake was away at school their little town was "discovered." First the gays, then the gourmets, then the tourists. On weekends, the restaurants and galleries were packed, and the line of cars stretched a mile out of town. Like all the locals, they bitched about it, but in the smug way of insiders. There were attempts to mobilize, but they bogged down in meetings or ran out of steam. Hard to get worked up when business is booming and your house is worth five times what you paid for it.

Buck ran a clean business. Not a bribe or kickback in a dozen years. Paid his taxes to the nickel and gave a man his money's worth. He didn't think about Lynnewood, except for Dexter. Kept his old life buried under layers of new. Still, there were moments. Once Peyton asked him to attend a conference with her in Atlanta, but he wriggled out of it at the last minute. He read about a fugitive from New York who was captured in a Sausalito bar after 28 years, and it gnawed at him for months. He'd done a good job of covering his tracks, but he worried about the chance encounter. As he passed into middle age, he took comfort in knowing that his old friends wouldn't recognize him. With his white hair and prosperous paunch, he looked more Rotarian than robber, and he welcomed each change like a man growing younger.

He knew nothing of his mother and sisters back in Georgia. Couldn't say if they were alive or dead. It pained him to think he would never see them again, but that was the price, and he was willing to pay it.

The hardest thing was keeping it all from Peyton. When they'd met he'd told her he was from South Carolina, but that his family moved around a lot. Different towns and schools to explain away his lack of friends. Along the line, his folks had died and he'd come out here. A simple story and easy to dodge around, if a bit too sketchy to pass for a past. For a while he tried fabricating recollections, or altering events, but he saw the trouble that would come of it and kept the story straight. The few times Peyton had pressed him, he'd steered her questions into a fight.

He always thought he would tell her someday, but time went by, and he never did.

Jake graduated Stanford at the top of his class. For most of a year, he tripped around Europe, then took his master's at the Sorbonne. Of all the things that had happened to Buck, this was the one nobody could touch: his son, the scholar, man of the world. Few in his family had even made it through high school, and most had never left the state. Jake could speak three languages and quote Voltaire. Buck's mother had it wrong all along. It was ignorance, not misfortune that ran in the blood. Jake was living proof. When he'd walked away from Lynnewood, Buck walked away from a world of trouble, and now that world had ceased to exist.

On their twentieth anniversary, Buck took Peyton to Paris to visit Jake. They booked a top floor apartment on Isle St. Louis with a terrace view that was worth the price alone. The strange course of his life never seemed so dear as it did looking out on the city lights. Every day was a gift, and he knew he'd done his best with the cards that were dealt him. It wasn't getting caught that scared him. It's where he would be if he had served his time. If he'd done a single thing differently, or made one wrong move. His life had been a good one, and he had Dexter to thank for that.

"I'm gonna save you, little dick. I'm gonna teach you how to use the only two things you got." He does the preacher routine, pacing and waving his hands. *"I'm gonna show you how to live a life."*

"These two things you say I got. ... What are they?"

Dexter turns on those headlight eyes. "You got a brain. I know you got a brain cause you knew what my origami was. Ain't no stupid people know about origami."

"What's the other?"

"Your sorry white ass. Wouldn't waste my time on no brother." Dexter drops into a crouch. "Too many times a brain does a nigger no good."

"What do you know about living a life, anyway?"

"When I came here I didn't know shit, but time is time. You can put it to use."

"In here? Not exactly role model city, homes."

"Save it, little dick. You ain't Black, and you ain't bad. It's why I picked you."

"What do you know about my dick?"

"It's white ain't it?"

"You got the wrong guy, Dexter."

"You're not listening to me. I'm gonna make you the right guy. I'm gonna teach you everything you got to know, and then I'm gonna set you free."

"Why?"

Dexter sits with his arms around his knees staring down between his legs.

"Let's just say it's research."

"I think I'll pass, Dexter"

Again the headlights, high beam this time.

"Ain't no pass, boy. You're the one."

That first night in Paris, they met Jake for drinks at an outdoor bistro. The kid was a marvel, chatting with the waiter, flirting with barmaid, speaking of things they knew nothing about. After two days of sightseeing, Buck was happy just to watch him work. It was what he'd been waiting for. A chance to revel in it. That his sorry line could have made this leap was inconceivable. And yet there he was. The blood of his blood.

"So I had to fly to Philadelphia to see the Soutine," Jake was saying. "This Doctor Barnes had more artistic vision than all the curators of Europe."

"And more than a little luck, sounds to me."

"Not luck, Dad. He was absolutely passionate, and his taste was clairvoyant. Monet, Picasso, Cezanne. Do you know there are more Cezannes in Philadelphia then there are in Paris?"

Buck did not. What he knew about art could fit on a postcard, but he never tired of listening to Jake.

"It makes me nervous to think of you flying all over the place." Peyton eyed him over the rim of her wine glass.

"It's not so bad mom. The customs people are very accommodating."

"So did you see it? The Soutine?" Buck steered him back to the subject.

"Yes, and it was the strangest thing. Barnes stressed that the paintings should be accessible, so there are no barriers. I was standing as close to it as I am to you." Jake faded slightly at the thought. "Too close to process the effect, the depth of field, the distortion of light."

To live a life, Buck thought to himself.

"Soutine's style is very distinctive. Almost as if he used a trowel instead of a brush. The surface of his painting is like a relief map, sharp ridges and depressions, as much textural as visual. It was all I could do not to … "

"Touch it?" Peyton filled in the blank.

"Worse. I wanted to pick off a piece of it. It would be easy enough. Just take my fingernail, and snap!"

"But you didn't."

"It was the fear of getting caught that restrained me. I would be disgraced, so I didn't dare. But I wanted to."

"But why?"

"It's difficult to explain, mom. These paintings are creations. You take the basic elements, canvas, paint, put them in the hands of a genius, and he brings them to life. It's a physical transformation, a product of the artist's hand. But without the elements there is no painting. He must work with them, touch them, breathe them in. It is the accumulation of paint that we see, after all. Stroke upon stroke directly applied. A series of movements, combining one element with the other.

The intimacy of man and material. The painting, as striking as it may be, is merely the result."

"Like French cooking," Buck grinned like an idiot.

"Exactly. You can taste the food, and you can see the painting but you're not part of the creation. Only the artist and the elements have a role. And since the artist is dead … "

Peyton looked to Buck. "You have only the elements."

"Exactement, Mom. Right there for the taking, a tiny paint chip. Who would miss it?"

Buck would bet he had it on him.

They had been back from Paris for less than a month when Buck suffered his first dizzy spell. He was leading a young couple through their basement when his vision began to blur. To the couple's astonishment, he walked face first into a support beam, nearly knocking himself unconscious. The second time, he was having a beer in Juanita's, and had to grab ahold of the bar to keep from collapsing. At first he wrote it off as age, but a blackout at the wheel argued against it.

Got the CAT scan, got the MRI, and prayed to God he would be alright. A few days later, they called him in, and he saw in their faces it wasn't good. They'd found a tumor in the brain stem. Small but inoperable. Four to six months was the best they could do. Buck just sat there, crunching the numbers. Multiplied four times thirty, then six times thirty, then rewound the calendar to get an idea. The PA system crackled in the hallway, and laughing voices passed the door. Sixteen weeks to the end of the story. After nearly three decades, his luck had run out.

"A smart man don't do no crime. At least crime you got to pay for. Only way to pay is with your life. One day at a time. A smart man knows how much you got to rob and steal to make a living. Ain't never been worth the effort. The more you steal, the more they catch you."

Dexter rolls his collar up against the wind. From the top of the bleachers they can see across the clearing to the edge of the swamp. Premium seats, off limits to lightweights, but he's there with Dexter so everything's cool.

"Tell me, Dex. If I'm so smart, how come I'm in here?"

He just shakes his head. "Never said you was smart, little dick. I said you got a brain. Look at Leon down there." They watch the big man cross the yard. "Old Leon robbed more banks than Jesse James, but the last time they caught him he was sleeping in a car. A smart man don't sleep in no damn car."

"Old Leon's dumb as a stump."

"Check it out." Dexter stares out over the wall. "If you was to find yourself alone by those trees with nothing but the clothes on your back, what would you do?"

"Run like hell and boost the first car I saw."

"Just what Leon did. Big Daddy had him hog tied in the hole before the sun came up." Dexter yanks a knit cap from his pocket and pulls it down over his head.

"How did he do it? Get out, I mean."

"Prison's like a living thing. Runs on habit, mostly. Sooner or later someone gets careless. A smart man is always ready." Dexter gives a wave to the watchtower. The guard leans out and flips him the finger.

"They're gonna be watching you now, boy," Dexter chuckles. "I was you, I'd watch my step."

"You say you know a way out of here. How come you don't go yourself?"

"Another three years, and I'm free and clear. No way I'm gonna fuck that up."

"What about me, Dexter? I'm up for parole at the end of the year."

Dexter laughs out loud at this one.

"That boy that died, how old was he?"

"I had nothing to do with that."

"Seventeen? Eighteen? They'll have the whole damn family down here tearing their hair out. You ain't going no place, son."

He doesn't say anything. Keeps watching those trees, seeing himself out there.

Buck told no one about the tumor. He kept it secret to spare Peyton and postpone the burden of sympathy, and because saying the words would make it so. He'd seen how friends react to a death sentence. The deference, the strained exchanges, the not so gradual phasing out. He'd been guilty of it himself. When Jack Walters' liver shut down, he hardly saw him towards the end. To keep his secret, Buck went for treatment at a Richmond clinic and filled his prescriptions at the hospital pharmacy. He could feel the days slipping by, but he did his best to act like himself. Once word got out, there was no taking it back.

Just before Thanksgiving, Jake called to say he was getting married. The girl's name was Genevieve, and the wedding was scheduled for the last Saturday in June. Peyton booked a flight the very next day, round trip for two with a weekend in London. She'd spent a year in England when she was in college, and couldn't wait to show Buck around.

"I wish it was already June," she grumbled.

"It'll be here before you know it," he said, and tried to sound cheerful. Depending on the doctor, he'd be gone a week to two months by then.

By Christmas he'd dropped twenty pounds, and the dizzy spells were taking a toll. He cut back on his workload, but doctored his schedule so Peyton wouldn't notice. Used the time to put his affairs in order, and made arrangement to sell the business. When Peyton voiced concern over his weight loss, he told her he was getting in shape. Even joined a gym to back it up. Then came the migraines. Once or twice a week in the beginning, but increasing in frequency and duration as the weeks passed. Pain so fierce he lay in bed weeping quietly. Peyton beside him, out like a light.

He told her on a Sunday morning. She was in bed stroking the cat, watching the sun inch down the window. A thin coat of ice melting in the time it took him. Not looking at her. Speaking in a level voice. Gave it to her straight, then rocked her in his arms as she fell to pieces.

"California? I don't even know how to get to California!"

"That's the point, little. They'll be turning over every rock in your skunky old town while you're three times zones away laying on the beach."

"I don't know anybody out there."

"Point number two."

"But why California?"

"Highest per capita income. You go where the money is. It's the de facto state where they got no niggers and they pride themselves on their tolerance."

"So I go three freakin' time zones so folks will be nice to me?"

"There you go."

"I can go to Memphis for that. What's the real reason, Dexter?"

"You ain't ready for the real reason. But I got time, so I'll tell you anyway. Three thousand wetbacks a week. This is a state that's not big on documentation. Get you some I.D. and you're a citizen. Think about it, man. No sheet, no priors."

He thinks about it.

"Number three, hippies and homos bookin' in by the boatload. These are folks with a program, and soon, they'll be running things. Which brings me to four. Political climate. Don't look at me like that, cracker. You got things to consider."

"Political climate? What the fuck?"

"Consider this. They got more liberal guilt in the Bay Area than they know what to do with. They're just dying to help." Dexter gives him a grin. *"Throw yourself on their mercy, son."*

"Sounds like I'm back in the courtroom."

"You ever hear of a one-time loser? Which brings us to number ..."

"Five?"

"Five. No death penalty in California. They catch you out there, and you best kill somebody, cause Mr. Big Daddy will be waiting for your ass."

"You don't seem to think much of my chances."

"Without me, you got no chance. Do what I say, and you walk away. Not just from Lynnewood, from all of it. The robbing and fixing, the whole sorry mess."

"I just want out. I don't need to be born ag -."

Dexter has him pinned to the wall before he can finish. Those headlight eyes fused to his own. His words coming in a low even tone.

"I told you it's been decided. You bail on me, and I set the dogs lose. You got that? Fuck up, and there's no safe place for you. That's a promise, little dick."

Buck nods furiously, and Dex lets him go. This isn't even about him. He felt it in the force of Dexter's grip. Not fury, but restraint. The man could snap his head off in a heartbeat.

"You meet me here every day. You hear what I tell you, and you take it to heart."

"It's Big Daddy, ain't it."

"Six breaks in sixteen years, all but one of em back in a week. All of them dead within the year. The man takes it personally."

"And the one?"

"Dogs got him at edge of those trees."

"Killed him?"

"Not before tearing him limb from limb. Daddy left him out there for two days."

Dexter gives him a couple of light slaps.

"Remember what I said about watching your step. They see us together and they're bound to start thinking. Can't be helped, y'understand?"

The inmate has no right to privacy. They take his name and give him a number, and if you know the number, you can always find him. If you don't know, you can call and ask for it. Doesn't matter who you are - a vengeful victim, a long lost relative, a lawyer looking to make a deal. The inmates' where-abouts are a matter of record.

Buck landed in Tampa on the first day of spring train-ing. The first pennant race that would finish without him. He rented a car and a cheap hotel room, and passed the night in a morphine haze. In the morning, he showered and shaved, put on clean clothes, and studied himself in the bathroom mirror. The face of a stranger stared back. Not just older, but worn out, lined with worry. Skin the color of damp concrete. He'd stopped all treatments weeks ago out of vanity and despair. He was thin, but far from emaciated. The tumor would kill him before he wasted away.

On the drive to Lynnewood, he thought about Peyton. Tried to imagine how she'd feel when she learned the truth. Would she judge him by their years together, or would the depth of his deception prove overwhelming? Both seemed likely. His life with her was already fading, as if distance was a measure of time. Or was the proximity of his old life working a change? The loss of one adding to the other. Peyton's love was the thing he could count on. How much did she count on him being Buck?

He tried putting himself in her place, but it was like trying to see through a prison wall. Whatever he'd done would be irrevocable. For Payton, for Jake and for all things Clayton. A borrowed name with a life of its own, a hooker's gift to a junkie thief.

His visit was scheduled for 10:00 am. He bought a road map at a convenience store, and traced his route with a magic marker. Strange to spend two years in a place, and still not know how to get there. He'd told them he was an insurance investigator tracking a stolen painting. The name Dexter Gannon had surfaced in an interview. He'd worked out the story in great detail, even had business cards and a letter of reference with a notarized seal. It was a good story, but hardly necessary. In the end they didn't give a damn. The inmate Gannon was still in confinement, and Big Daddy Mercer still ran the show.

At half past nine he pulled off in a cutout overlooking the complex. There were new buildings and ill-fitting additions, but the main structure, the towers and the distant swamp, were as they had been. He watched a group of prisoners killing time in the yard, fifty men clumped in five and tens. A basketball game going despite the heat. He saw a single figure high in the bleachers, but too far away to make out his face. Dexter would be close to seventy, and Buck wondered if he'd been there the whole time. If so, it was easy to figure why.

The prisoners glared as he drove through the gate. A cage now contained the laundry exhaust fan housing, and the tin shed where Dexter had stashed the bolt cutter had been removed. He parked the car in the space marked for visitors, and signed his name to the entry log. His voice was even, his hands steady. A dying man with nothing to lose.

They led Dexter in through an unmarked door. His hair was speckled with white, and he'd grown a moustache, but he still looked solid, still had the swagger. He took his seat and stared hard at Buck, then leaned forward and picked up the phone.

"What do you want?"

Buck gave a glance to the guards, but they paid him no mind.

"Can they hear what I'm saying?" he asked.

Dexter said nothing.

"It's me. Little dick."

His face barely registered the news, and for a second, Buck wondered if he'd somehow forgotten. But then a frown turned the corners of his mouth, and he looked away, as if embarrassed.

"I'll be damned," he said softly, then shook his head, and said it again. "I'll be damned."

"What do you think, man?"

Dexter just kept shaking his head. "I think you better get the fuck outa here before I do something illegal."

"How you been?"

Dexter leaned in and turned on the high beams. "I'm not playin with you, boy. One word to those bulls over there, and you're back on the inside lookin out."

"That's the whole point."

"I guess I was wrong about the brain."

"You saved my life, Dexter. Now it's my turn."

"I'm done here," he said, and moved to hang up.

"Wait," a quick check of the guards. "It's over for me, OK?"

"Say what you mean, boy. I'm a busy man."

"Cancer. It's terminal." Buck gave him a shrug. "No possibility of parole."

The high beams flickered, then died. Dexter looked instantly ten years older.

"I'm sorry to hear that."

"Don't be. I lived a life. That's what it was all about, right?"

The old con settled back in his chair, ran a hand over his face. "Part of it."

"Now we take care of the other part."

"The other part took care of itself."

"Big Daddy took it hard?"

"Still takin' it hard. Got so worked up he had himself a stroke. Must be fifteen years ago now. Been walkin' with a cane ever since. Like I told you, with him, it's personal."

Buck smiled until Dexter smiled back.

"Let's finish him off, Dex."

"You don't know what you're saying."

"You have a lawyer, right?"

"On a thirty year retainer?"

"OK, we get you one. You go to Big Daddy with a deal. An even-up swap. You go home, he gets a dead man. What could be sweeter?"

Dexter laughed.

"Hey Dex, what do you have to lose?"

"Look around you, little. This is my home. They say I've been institutionalized. You know what that means?"

"Fuck what they say. I'm getting you out."

"I been out. First time was for three months back in '74. The last time was two years back. I didn't last a week."

"Big Daddy?"

"Shiiiit. He didn't have nothin to do with it. Comes a point where you can't make it outside."

"That's bullshit, and you know it."

"Tell me something, little. You have kids?"

"A boy. Get this, he lives in Paris."

Dexter eyes glazed over, and for a moment Buck thought maybe he'd killed him.

"Got me two little girls." His voice came from a distance. "Course, I suspect they ain't so little anymore. It happened during my three-month vacation. Twins, little! Ain't that a bitch?"

"You seen them?"

"Never laid eyes on 'em."

"This will be your chance."

"I wouldn't do that to 'em. Whatever life they got, they don't need me in it."

"So you're just gonna lay up here and die."

"In time. First, I gotta outlive the man."

"You can't be serious." Buck felt a pounding above the cords of his neck, spreading almost to his ears. He had to end this quickly if he hoped to make the motel.

"Listen Dexter, promise me you'll think about it."

"Nothing to think about. Too late to assimilate. That's what the old timers say. Out there, you see all the million ways you fucked up. The world just rubs your face in it." Dexter looked away. "If it makes you feel any better, there ain't a day goes by I don't think of you, little. Hell, I knew you could be dead or doing time, but there was always the chance you made it. Sometimes it was the only thing that kept me going."

Buck held on to the edge of the table as a wave of nausea passed.

"Easy, son."

"Yeah. Listen. Can I call you?"

"Go on home. Leave an old nigger alone."

Dexter smiled until Buck smiled back.

"You lived a life, didn't you, little?"

"That I did, Dexter."

"I'll see you soon. You'll tell me all about it."

"I believe I will."

He takes the injection, then counts the seconds. In the moment between agony and oblivion, he dreams he is on a train looking out on a full moon. A private compartment like the one they took to Canada years ago. The trees across the Straits shining silver, light reflected in a jagged line across the water. He hears music playing in the next compartment. The end of a tenor solo he knows by heart. Giving way to a trumpet's trill, high and sweet, sliding to a whisper, a famous jazzman playing the blues.

They pass the water tower, the lumberyard, and the soft light from Juanita's back porch. He sees Payton waiting for him at the wrought iron table, searching the windows, straining for a look at her boy, Buck. The trumpet falls silent. He doesn't move, just lets the sight of her fill him up.

AUTHOR BIO

Tom Larsen lives in the Pennsport section of South Philadelphia, home to Mummers, Flyers and that "screw you" slant that made this city great. For a writer auditioning characters, the 19148 zip is a casting gold mine. Tom worked as a journeyman pressman for thirty years before scrapping it all for the writer's life. His work has appeared in Raritan, The Los Angeles Review, Philadelphia Stories Magazine, New Millennium Writing and Best American Mystery Stories